‖‖‖‖‖‖‖ ‖‖‖‖‖‖
◁ P9-CQM-849

"You Were Beautiful That Night," Alec Said, Giving Her Figure A Slow Once-Over.

Charlotte couldn't contain herself. "I was twenty-two that night."

"You didn't have to take the key."

"I was confused." It had taken her a moment to realize the card he'd handed her was a hotel room key.

"You were tempted."

"I'd known you for two minutes." Other women might be tempted by a dashing aristocrat with money to burn, but Charlotte wasn't interested in a fling.

"I'd been watching you for a lot longer than two minutes. You were attractive. You seemed interesting and intelligent, and by the way you were making all those other men laugh, I knew you had a sense of humor."

"Giving me your room key was supposed to be funny?"

"I wanted to get to know you better."

"It didn't occur to you to ask me for coffee?"

"I'm not a patient man."

* * *

Don't miss the exclusive in-book short story by
USA TODAY **bestselling author Maureen Child**
after the last page of
Transformed Into the Frenchman's Mistress!

Dear Reader,

Is there anything more romantic than a chateau in the south of France, with picturesque gardens, a well-stocked wine cellar and hot hero? And who doesn't love the thought of being whisked away to Paris, Rome and London in a private jet?

French aristocrat Alec Montcalm has it all: the looks, the pedigree, the money and all those gorgeous women. And Charlotte Hudson doesn't trust him for a single second. Unfortunately, the favor she's forced to ask is a test of her loyalty to her family. It's a favor Alec is willing to grant her—for a price.

I hope you enjoy the newest installment in the Hudsons' saga!

Barbara Dunlop

BARBARA DUNLOP

TRANSFORMED INTO THE FRENCHMAN'S MISTRESS

Silhouette®

Desire

Published by Silhouette Books
America's Publisher of Contemporary Romance

If you purchased this book without a cover you should be aware that this book is stolen property. It was reported as "unsold and destroyed" to the publisher, and neither the author nor the publisher has received any payment for this "stripped book."

Special thanks and acknowledgments to Barbara Dunlop for her contribution to The Hudsons of Beverly Hills series.

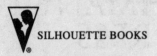

SILHOUETTE BOOKS

ISBN-13: 978-0-373-76929-2
ISBN-10:   0-373-76929-6

Recycling programs
for this product may
not exist in your area.

TRANSFORMED INTO THE FRENCHMAN'S MISTRESS

Copyright © 2009 by Harlequin Books S.A.

All rights reserved. Except for use in any review, the reproduction or utilization of this work in whole or in part in any form by any electronic, mechanical or other means, now known or hereafter invented, including xerography, photocopying and recording, or in any information storage or retrieval system, is forbidden without the written permission of the editorial office, Silhouette Books, 233 Broadway, New York, NY 10279 U.S.A.

This is a work of fiction. Names, characters, places and incidents are either the product of the author's imagination or are used fictitiously, and any resemblance to actual persons, living or dead, business establishments, events or locales is entirely coincidental.

This edition published by arrangement with Harlequin Books S.A.

® and TM are trademarks of Harlequin Books S.A., used under license. Trademarks indicated with ® are registered in the United States Patent and Trademark Office, the Canadian Trade Marks Office and in other countries.

Visit Silhouette Books at www.eHarlequin.com

Printed in U.S.A.

Books by Barbara Dunlop

Silhouette Desire

Thunderbolt over Texas #1704
Marriage Terms #1741
The Billionaire's Bidding #1793
The Billionaire Who Bought Christmas #1836
Beauty and the Billionaire #1853
Marriage, Manhattan Style #1897
Transformed Into the Frenchman's Mistress #1929

BARBARA DUNLOP

is a bestselling, award-winning author of numerous novels for Harlequin and Silhouette Books. Her books regularly hit bestseller lists for series romance, and she has twice been short-listed for the Romance Writers of America's RITA® Award.

Barbara lives in a log house in the Yukon Territory, where the bears outnumber people and moose browse the front yard. By day, she works as the Yukon's Film Commissioner. By night, she pens romance novels in front of a roaring fire. Visit her Web site at www.barbaradunlop.com.

For Susie Ross

One

Slightly windblown, and more than a little jet-lagged, Charlotte Hudson found herself in France. A phone call from her brother, Jack, yesterday had cut short her tour with their grandfather, Ambassador Edmond Cassettes. The diplomatic contingent had been in New Orleans, where Charlotte and the ambassador were being wined, dined and entertained by the governor, a couple of senators and every Louisiana mayor with aspirations of doing business with the wealthy Mediterranean nation of Monte Allegro.

Then Jack had called, and now she was in Provence, pulling up to the Montcalm family château with a favor to ask. Her college friend Raine would be surprised to see her, but Charlotte was couting on Raine's good nature to help her secure the favor. It was the first time her brother, or anyone on the Hudson side of the family, had included her in Hudson Pictures' film-making business. And she desperately wanted to impress.

Charlotte had been raised in Europe by her maternal grandparents, while Jack was raised an ocean away in Hollywood by the Hudsons. She mad met the film-making dynasty of a family on only a couple of occasions. They were perfectly polite to her, but it was clear they were close-knit, and she was very much the outsider.

But now, terminally ill matriarch Lillian Hudson was determined to honor her late husband's wishes by having Hudson Pictures bring their wartime romance to the big screen. The entire family had rallied around the project and decreed Château Montcalm was the perfect location.

Charlotte finally had a chance to participate in the Hudsons' world.

She drew a breath, giving her straight skirt and matching ivory blazer a final tug as she approached the main doors of the Montcalm's stately, three-story stone mansion. The doors were intimidating oversize planked walnut, inset with vintage beveled windows. The château was old-world and impressive. She knew it had been in the Montcalm family for a dozen generations, ever since some fiery warlord of a Montcalm ancestor had taken it in battle. Her friend Raine had quite the pedigree.

Charlotte took a breath and reached for the ornate doorbell, waiting only a moment until a formally dressed butler drew the door wide, his expression a study in formality and courtesy.

"*Bonjour, madame.*"

"Bonjour," Charlotte returned. "I'm looking for Raine Montcalm."

The man paused while he considered Charlotte's appearance. "Do you have an appointment?"

Charlotte shook her head. "I'm Charlotte Hudson. Raine and I are friends. We were together at Oxford."

"Mademoiselle Montcalm is unavailable."

"But—"

"I do apologize."

"Could you at least tell her I'm here?" She hoped Raine would become available if she heard Charlotte's name.

"The mademoiselle is not currently in residence."

Charlotte struggled to decide if she was getting the brush-off. "She's really not here?"

He didn't answer, but his expression became crisper and even more formal, if that was possible.

"Because, if you could just let her know—"

"A problem, Henri?" came a gravelly, masculine voice.

Oh no. Not Alec.

"Non, monsieur."

Charlotte reflexively drew back as a tall, aristocratically handsome man moved into the doorway, displacing the butler. Raine's brother was supposed to be in London. Charltte had seen his picture in the tabloids just yesterday, dancing at some posh nightclub on Whitehall.

"I'm afraid Raine's away on—" He suddenly stopped speaking. A wolfish smile grew on his lips. "Charlotte Hudson."

She didn't answer.

"Thank you, Henri." Alec's dismissal was polite but clear, his gaze never leaving Charlotte.

As the butler drew back, Alec leaned indolently against the doorjamb. He wore a charcoal Caraceni suit, a classic white shirt and a dark silk tie that was scattered with bright red flecks. The flecks, it seemed, were miniatures of the Montcalm family crest, painstakingly embroidered into the fabric.

Her heart pounding with a mixture of awareness and trepidation, Charlotte decided to bluff. She held out her hand and gave him a breezy smile. "I don't believe we've been formally introduced."

At least that part wasn't a lie. There'd been nothing remotely formal about their one and only meeting. It had been humiliating, and her only defense was to pretend she'd forgotten all about it.

"Oh, we've been introduced, Ms. Hudson." His warm, callused hand closed over hers, sending a shiver along her spine.

She painstakingly schooled her features, raising her brow in question.

"Three years ago." He cocked his head to one side, clearly challenging her to acknowledge him.

She held her ground.

"The *Ottobrate Ballo* in Rome," he continued, eyes mocking. "I asked you to dance."

He'd done a lot more than ask. He'd nearly derailed her career in under five minutes.

Rome had been one of her first official assignments as her grandfather's executive assistant. Becoming his official E.A. had been a big step for her, and she'd been nervous all night, anxious to do well.

Alec's smile widened as he watched her expression. "It's etched very firmly in *my* mind," he told her.

"I don't—"

"Sure you do," he countered softly, and they both knew he was right. "And you liked it."

Too true.

"But then Ambassador Cassettes stepped in."

Thank goodness for her grandfather.

"Charlotte?" Alec prompted.

She pretended she'd only just remembered. "You tried to give me your room key," she accused with a stern frown.

"And you took it."

"I didn't know what it was." She'd been twenty-two years old, a neophyte on the diplomatic circuit, and he'd been right there, poised to take advantage of her.

He chuckled his disbelief, and she glared at him.

Then he sobered. "You were beautiful that night." His gaze went soft as he gave her figure a slow once-over.

She couldn't keep the outrage from her tone. "I was twenty-two that night."

His shoulders went up in a careless shrug. "You didn't have to take the key."

"I was confused." It truly had taken her a moment to realize the card he'd handed her was a hotel room key.

"I think you were tempted."

Her brain warned her mouth to shut up. But her emotions overrode the instruction. "I'd known you for two minutes." Other women might be tempted by a dashing, urbane aristocrat with money to burn, but Charlotte wasn't interested in a fling.

"I'd been watching you for a lot longer than two minutes."

His words caused her thoughts to stumble. He'd

been watching her? In a complimentary way, or in a creepy, stalker sort of way?

He moved subtly closer. "You were attractive. You seemed interesting and intelligent, and by the way you were making all those other men laugh, I knew you had a sense of humor."

"Giving me your room key was supposed to be funny?"

His brown eyes turned to molten chocolate. "Not at all. The ball was ending. I wanted to get to know you better."

Charlotte couldn't believe his gall. Aside from being young and naive, she'd been on official business that night, and she'd never dishonor her grandfather nor the ambassador's office by leaving the party with a strange man, particularly a man with Alec Montcalm's reputation. He was still one of France's most notorious bachelors. His dates were lucky to stay out of the tabloids.

"It didn't occur to you to ask me for coffee?" she asked tartly.

"I'm not a patient man." He paused, and she checked an impulse to gaze into his dark eyes, or to contemplate that rakish slash of a mouth, or the tilt of his square chin. Which left her his nose—straight, aristocratic, slightly flared, as if he was drinking in her scent.

He continued speaking. "The direct approach is sometimes the most effective."

"You're telling me that room-key thing works?" She couldn't really be surprised. There had to be plenty of women who'd give their eye teeth to hop into Alec Montcalm's bed. Charlotte simply wasn't one of them. And she never would be.

His quirk of a smile confirmed her suspicions. But then he seemed to tire of the game. He straightened, his expression turning more businesslike. "In my sister's absence, is there anything I can do for you, Ms. Hudson?"

Charlotte instantly remembered her mission. She also realized she'd made a colossal error by arguing with him. She forced herself to calm down, to step back from the web of emotions he seemed to evoke, and to focus on the reason she'd come.

"When is Raine expected back?" she tried.

"Tuesday morning. She was called to a photo shoot on Malta for *Intérêt*."

Charlotte knew *Intérêt* was the Montcalm Corporation's fashion magazine, and Raine was editor-in-chief. Tuesday morning wasn't going to do it. Jack needed to know this weekend if he could send the film's location manager to Château Montcalm. Principal photography was set to start at the end of the summer, and they were already behind schedule.

Charlotte supposed she could fly to Malta and talk to Raine there. But she knew the magazine wouldn't call out the editor-in-chief unless there was a problem. The last thing she wanted to do was catch Raine at a stressful time. It wouldn't help her cause, and it wouldn't be fair to Raine.

That left Alec. She had *so* hoped to avoid asking him directly. But she wasn't in a position to be choosy.

She took a bracing breath. "There's something I'd like to discuss with you."

Alec's eyes instantly twinkled, and an anticipatory smile transformed his slash of a mouth.

Charlotte battled a spontaneous sexual reaction.

There was a reason women from Milan and Prague accepted his room key on the dance floor. The man was sexy as sin.

"Entrer," he offered, gesturing with his arm and making a small space between his body and the door for her to enter the foyer.

She hesitated, then took the invitation, brushing past him, a tingle invading her shoulder where it contacted his chest.

"Dinner is casual tonight," he told her. *"La pissaladière.* And I'll bring up a bottle of 1996 Montcalm *Maison Inouï* from the cellar."

"It's not that kind of a discussion," she warned, turning back to face him. Bringing out the big guns from his family's winery wasn't going to make her fall into his bed.

"You're in Provence," he countered smoothly, closing the door. "Everything is that kind of a discussion."

She blinked to adjust her eyes to the interior light. "This is business."

"I understand." But his expression didn't change.

"Do you?"

"Absolument."

She didn't believe him for a second. But she had no choice but to stay for dinner. Jack needed the location. She needed the credibility with the Hudson family. And she wasn't about to blow this chance.

Alec had been handed a second chance.

Three long years later, the sexy woman he'd admired across the dance floor was in his kitchen, looking sexier than ever. If he'd known Raine's friend Charlotte and his *Ottobrate Ballo* Charlotte were one and the same, he'd have made this happen a whole lot sooner. But patience was good. Anticipation was good.

And now, gazing at her crystal-clear blue eyes, her dark lashes, her full lips and porcelain-smooth skin, he was glad he'd waited. Her neck was long and graceful, decorated with a delicate, moon-shaped diamond and gold pendant that telegraphed taste rather than extravagance. The suit's skirt fit her like a glove, emphasizing the curve of her waist, the flare of her hips and her long, sleek, toned legs that ended in a pair of sexy heels.

On the butcher-block island in the terra-cotta tiled kitchen, he popped the cork on the *Maison Inouï*. It was his family's signature label, their finest vintage, bottles he saved for very special occasions.

He reached up to the hanging rack, sliding off a pair of crystal red-wine goblets.

Having initially gazed around with interest, Charlotte was now standing uncertainly at the center of the large room.

He nodded to one of the low-backed bar stools on the opposite side of the island. "Hop up."

She hesitated for a split second, but then slipped gracefully into the leather-upholstered seat, setting her small clutch bag on the lip of the counter.

"Thank you," she said primly as he placed one of the glasses of wine in front of her.

Alec remembered that intriguing expression, the shield of formality, covering what he was certain was a fiery rebel, chafing beneath the bounds of propriety. He'd tried to test the theory in Rome, but her grandfather, the watchful ambassador, had stopped him cold.

Back then, he'd shrugged the disappointment off

philosophically. Women came; women went. Sometimes it worked out. Sometimes it didn't.

He lifted his wineglass, swirling the small measure of wine, taking an experimental sip and letting the deep, sweet, woodsy flavor of the wine glide over his tongue.

Sometimes a man got another chance.

The wine was perfect, so he filled their glasses.

Charlotte tasted hers, and her eyes went wide with the experience. "Nice," she admitted with respect.

"From our vineyard in Bordeaux."

"I'm impressed."

He smiled in satisfaction at her reaction.

"Not *that* impressed," she drawled.

"That was pride of craftsmanship," he told her.

"My mistake." But her sea-foam eyes told him she knew it was lust.

Of course it was. But not a problem. He'd back off and let her relax.

"La pissaladière," he decreed, retrieving a steel mixing bowl from beneath the countertop. He then assembled flour, yeast, sugar and olive oil.

She watched wordlessly for a few moments. "You can cook?"

"Oui. Of course." He sprinkled sugar into the bottom of the bowl, adding the yeast and a measure of water. French children learned to bake almost before they learned to walk.

"You do your own cooking?" she pressed in obvious surprise.

"Sometimes." He nodded to her wineglass. "Enjoy. Relax. Tell me what you wanted to talk about."

The invitation seemed to sober her, and she took a slow sip of the wine.

Stalling.

Interesting.

"That is one exceedingly fine wine," she commented.

"I applaud your good taste, *mademoiselle*," he told her honestly. Then he retrieved a heavy skillet and drizzled olive oil into the bottom.

"You've lived here a long time?" she asked. Her gaze was on her wineglass as she rubbed her thumb and forefinger over the stem.

He watched the motion for a moment. "I was born here."

"In Provence or in the château?"

"In the hospital in Castres."

"Oh." She nodded then turned silent.

"Is that what you wanted to ask me?"

"Not exactly." Her white teeth came down on her bottom lip. "My family in America…the Hudsons. They make movies."

"You don't say," he drawled. A person would have to be dead not to know of Hudson Pictures. Their awards were numerous, their reputation stellar and they'd launched the careers of half the Hollywood elite.

"I wasn't sure you knew," she defended. "They're successful in America, but—"

"You're far too modest."

"It's not like I had anything to do with it." She flicked back her hair, gaze still focused on the burgundy wine. "They're filming a new movie."

"Just one?"

That made her look up. "A special one."

"I see."

"I don't…." She glanced around the spacious kitchen.

Alec set down his chopping knife. "Is it getting any easier with these delay tactics?"

"I'm not—" Then she caught his eyes and sighed. "I really was hoping you'd be Raine."

"Sorry."

"Not as sorry as I am." Then she gave her head a little shake. "I didn't mean that the way it sounded."

If she didn't look so serious, he might have laughed. "Is it some kind of women's thing?"

"*No.*"

"Boyfriend break up with you?" That wouldn't be such a bad thing. She could stay here while she got over the guy. And Alec would be on hand to lend a sympathetic ear, or shoulder, or anything else that was required.

"No," she said. "It's not that."

Too bad. "Am I likely to guess?"

She fought a half smile and shook her head.

He picked up the knife, bringing it down to chop off the stem of an onion. "Then shall we get on with it?"

"You're not making this easy."

He chopped again. "Well, it's not from the lack of trying."

Her lips compressed, then her shoulders drooped. "Okay, now there's been too much buildup."

He rinsed his hands in the small square sink in the middle of the island. "*You,*" he enunciated, "are impossible."

"Fine." She braced her hands on the countertop. "Here goes. The Hudsons would like to use your château as a movie set." She clamped her jaw and waited for his reaction.

Alec stilled.

Was she joking?

Was she crazy?

He'd spent years avoiding the press—years of fighting tooth and nail for a scrap of privacy. To invite a movie crew, cameras, actors, an entire Hollywood cartel into his home for weeks on end?

He gathered the thinly sliced onions onto the knife edge, then dumped them all at once in the hot olive oil. They hissed and sizzled, steam rising to the ceiling.

"No," he said, with absolute finality. There was not a chance in hell.

Okay, Charlotte had expected resistance. Alec wasn't going to say yes immediately. Who would? It was an inconvenience and a disruption in his life. She understood that.

"It's my grandparents' love story," she put in, trying to stress the significance of the film. "They met during the war. In occupied France."

Alec didn't say a word.

"All of Hudson Pictures' resources will be behind it." The quality would be unparalleled.

He lifted a spatula and stirred the sizzling onions.

"My grandmother was a cabaret performer, and they were secretly married under the noses of the Germans."

Alec looked up. "And this makes a difference how?"

"Cece Cassidy is attached to the project. It's sure to be a contender for best writer—"

"Like the screenwriter's the problem."

"Is it about money?" she probed. "They'd absolutely compensate you for the inconvenience. And they'd leave everything exactly as they found it. You wouldn't—"

"It's about my home not being a movie set."

"They wouldn't need your entire home." Charlotte

searched her brain for more ammunition. "You'd be able to stay in residence. Jack sent me a script breakdown. They'd need the kitchen, the great room, one of the libraries and a couple of bedrooms. Oh, and the grounds of course. They'd need the grounds. Maybe your back deck for one scene."

"And that's *all?*" Alec drawled, his sarcastic tone playing havoc with her confidence.

"I'm fairly sure that's all." She kept her voice even.

"They wouldn't need access to my private study? Or my bathroom?" he continued, voice going up. "Or maybe they'd like to take a peek inside—"

"You could designate some areas off-limits," she rushed in. "And you could even stay at one of your other houses during filming."

His eyes darkened, and he brandished the spatula like a weapon. "And give a pack of Hollywood hooligans free rein over my home?"

"It's not like they're some biker gang." Sure, some stars had a reputation for bad behavior, but the Hudson Pictures producers were very professional. And Raine was a friend. Charlotte wouldn't fill her house with a bunch of wild partiers.

"I never said they were."

"Then what is it?"

"Do you have *any* idea how hard I have to fight for privacy?"

"Well, maybe if you didn't—" She stopped herself.

"Yes?" he prompted, cocking his dark head to one side.

"Nothing." She shook her head. This was turning into enough of a disaster without her insulting him.

"I must insist," he said, seeming to grow even taller.

"We could cover any privacy concerns in the contract." She attempted to distract him. "You'd really have nothing to worry—"

"I'll decide what I worry about. Now what were you about to say?"

She gazed into his probing eyes. "I forgot."

He waited.

Her brain scrambled, but she couldn't for the life of her come up with a good lie.

Oh, hell. She might as well go for it. The battle was all but over, anyway. "Maybe if you didn't make yourself such an attractive target for the paparazzi."

He paused. "You're suggesting it's *my* fault?"

"You don't have to escort supermodels to every A-list party in Europe."

His brown eyes darkened to ebony. "You think a plain Jane on my arm would stop the gossip? You think a woman who didn't fit their mold would do *anything* but guarantee me the front page?"

Charlotte quickly realized he had a point. Being seen with anybody out of type would cause even more speculation. But he'd missed her point entirely. "You could skip the parties."

"I don't attend that many parties."

Charlotte scoffed out a laugh of disbelief.

He frowned at her. "How many did *you* attend last month? Last week? Lost count?"

In fact, she had. "That's different," she pointed out primly. "I was on business."

He gave the onions another stir and reduced the heat. "What is it you think I do at parties?"

He washed his hands while she thought about that. Then he retrieved a mesh bag of ripe tomatoes.

She tried to figure out if it was a trick question. "Dance with supermodels?" She stated the obvious.

"I make business contacts."

"With supermodels?"

He sliced through a tomato. "Would you rather I went stag? Danced with other men's dates?"

Charlotte wriggled forward on the high seat. "You're trying to tell me you *suffer* the attentions of supermodels in order to make business contacts?"

"I'm trying to tell you I like my privacy, and you shouldn't make assumptions about other people's lifestyles."

"Alec, you hand out hotel room keys on the dance floor." She knew from firsthand experience. He'd tried it with her.

His knife stilled.

She sat back, not even attempting to mask her satisfaction. "You are so busted."

"Really?" He resumed slicing. "Well, you are *so* not making a movie in my château."

Two

Round one had gone to Alec, and Charlotte had no choice but to back off and regroup as they moved to the veranda for dinner. The sizzling *pissaladière* was now on a round glass table between them.

Flickering light from the garden torches highlighted the planes and angles of his face, while the freshening breeze picked up the scents of lavender and thyme. He seemed relaxed enough. While the *pissaladière* had baked, their conversation had ranged from vacation spots to impressionist painters to the monetary policy of the European Union.

But now, it was time for round two.

"You could hide anything personal," she opened conversationally, transferring a slice of the delicate tomato pie to her plate. "You could stay out of sight. I doubt any of the crew would even know it was your château."

"Please," he drawled, lifting the silver serving spoon from her hand. "There's a big sign over the gate that says Château Montcalm."

"Take it down."

"My name is etched into five-hundred-year-old stone."

Right. "Surely you're not the only Montcalm in Provence."

"I'm the only one who makes the front page." He settled on two slices of the pie.

"I think you're overestimating your fame."

"I think you're overestimating your powers of persuasion."

"More wine?" she asked, topping off his glass while treating him to the brilliant smile her grandfather's image consultant had insisted she learn for photographs.

He watched the burgundy liquid rise in his crystal goblet. "It won't work, Charlotte."

She finished topping his glass. "What won't work?"

"I was weaned on *Maison Inouï*."

She feigned innocence. "You think I'm trying to get you drunk?"

"I think you're entirely too fixated on my château." He moved the bottle to one side so that his view of her was unobstructed. "What gives? There are plenty of other châteaus."

She tried to stay businesslike. But his mocha eyes glowed under the soft torchlight, making it look like he somehow cared.

"It's perfect for the story," she told him honestly, gazing around the estate. "The family thinks—"

"You're not even involved in the business."

Charlotte squared her shoulders. "I am a Hudson." She found herself battling a stupid but familiar sense of loneliness. Her Cassettes grandparents had given her a wonderful life, a dream life. If her heart had ached for her brother, Jack, in the dead of night, it was only because she'd been so young when they were separated.

"Charlotte?"

She blinked at Alec.

"There are many châteaus in Provence."

"He...*they* want this one."

"He?"

"The producers." She was doing this for the good of the film, not specifically for Jack.

"Something going on between you and the producers?"

"*No.*"

Alec gazed at her in silence. The wind kicked up a notch, and the stems of lavender rustled below them in the country garden.

"What?" she finally asked, battling an urge to squirm.

He lifted his wineglass. "You want it too bad."

She huffed out a breath. "I don't see why this has to be such a big thing. What do you want? What can we do? How can we persuade you to give up your precious privacy for six weeks?"

He sipped the wine, watching her intently. Then he set down the glass, running his thumb along the length of the stem.

"There is one thing I want." His molten eyes told her exactly what that one thing was.

"I am not sleeping with you to get a film location."

Alec tipped back his head and laughed.

Charlotte squirmed. Had she completely misread his signals? Made a colossal fool of herself?

No. She couldn't have been that far wrong. The man had once tried to give her his hotel room key.

"I'm not asking to sleep with you, Charlotte."

She took an unladylike swig of her own wine, struggling desperately not to blush in humiliation. "Well. Good. That's good."

He grinned. "Although, I definitely wouldn't say no if you—"

"Shut up."

He clamped his jaw.

She waited as long as she could stand.

"Fine. What is it—"

"Charlotte!" came Raine's delighted voice. She rushed through an open set of French doors, dropping her purse and a briefcase on a lounger. "Why didn't you *tell* me you were coming?"

She wore a slim, tailored black dress and charcoal stockings, and her high-heeled shoes clattered on the stone deck. Her dark hair was cut in a chic bob, and her bright red mouth was sliced in a smile of delight.

"The trip came up suddenly," said Charlotte, coming to her feet, as did Alec beside her. "But I thought you were away until Tuesday." She cursed her stupidity at rushing the conversation with Alec. If only she'd waited a few hours!

"I talked to Henri. He told me you were here." There was a clear admonishment in the tone.

But then they embraced in a tight hug, Raine laughing with delight in Charlotte's ear.

When they finally separated, Alec broke in. *"Bonsoir, ma soeur."*

Raine glanced over, feigning surprise. "Alec? I didn't see you there."

He shook his head and held out his arms.

She walked into a warm hug and an affectionate kiss for each cheek.

Watching them, regret twitched reflexively inside Charlotte. She glanced away, wishing she could have such an easy relationship with Jack.

"So," said Raine as she settled into the third chair. "What are we eating?" She sniffed at the *pissaladière*. Then she lifted the wine bottle, brows arching at the label. *"Très bon."*

"I know how to be a good host, even if you don't," said Alec.

"I didn't even know she was coming." Raine tipped the bottle up, and up. "It's empty."

Alec reached behind him, exchanging it for a full one while Raine helped herself to a slice of the pie.

"What are we talking about?" she asked, glancing from one to the other.

Alec deftly drilled into the wine cork. "Charlotte wants to use the château as a movie set."

Charlotte cringed at the bald statement.

But Raine looked intrigued. "Really?"

Charlotte nodded.

"That's *fantastic.*"

"I didn't say yes," Alec warned.

"Why on earth not?" asked Raine.

He popped the cork. "Because you interrupted us."

"But you were about to," she prompted.

"I was about to suggest a compromise."

Charlotte reminded herself it wasn't sex. Though there was still a nervous churning in her stomach.

What would Alec want? More important, what was she willing to give?

Not sex. No. Of course not. Still…

He continued speaking, and she forced herself to pay attention to the words. "I was going to say yes—"

Raine clapped her hands together in delight.

"Provided," Alec put in firmly, and Charlotte listened closely. "Provided we have an understanding that the third floor is off-limits. As is the south gallery."

"Done," Charlotte quickly answered, sticking out her hand to shake.

"Nobody goes in the rose garden." He didn't shake her hand.

She nodded vigorously. Easy. Piece of cake. According to Jack, landowners always had a list of stipulations.

"Or any of the outbuildings. Shooting stops by ten every night. My staff are *not* part of the production crew. And you stay in residence to make sure it goes smoothly."

"Abso—" Charlotte snapped her jaw shut, dropping her hand to the table. *"What?"*

"I don't want any extra work for my staff," he repeated.

"Not *that* part."

"It's perfect," Raine sang, grasping Charlotte's forearm in a friendly squeeze. "We can hang out, visit. It'll be like we're back in college."

"I can't move in," Charlotte protested. "I have a job back in Monte Allegro. My grandfather needs me. There's a summit in Athens on the twenty-fifth."

Alec pinned her with a look. "So you're willing to inconvenience *me,* but not yourself?"

"I'm not…" She gazed into his mocking eyes.

He raised a brow.

Instinct told her to grab the yes before he could change his mind. But here? With Alec? For weeks on end?

She thought back to the hotel room key, and to the way her stomach had quivered in daring anticipation for the split second when she'd thought about accepting it. She was older now, wiser, and she knew full well the importance of leading a perfectly circumspect life—one that didn't include a stint on the front page of the tabloids.

But the quiver was still there. And she knew that he knew. She could fight it all she wanted, intellectualize it all she wanted, but the bald truth was that she was attracted to the man. She and several thousand other women fantasized about a night in Alec Montcalm's bed. And Alec would take advantage of that in any way he could.

But then she pictured Jack's joy, her pride when she told him she'd succeeded. She thought about her grandmother and the whole Hudson clan. For once, she'd be part of the team.

"I'll stay," she told Alec.

Raine squealed in delight.

Alec reached for his wineglass, raising it in a mock toast while his dark, molten eyes told her the chase was on.

"They will *hound* you," said Kiefer, as he geared his mountain bike down for the incline.

"She's a friend of Raine's," Alec defended, following suit, putting more power to his pedals.

They were on a dirt road that wound along the ridgeline above the Montcalm estate. The tires bumped beneath Alec, and sweat began to form at his hairline as the sun cleared the eastern horizon, lighting up the river and the patchwork of fields and woods below.

"So?" Kiefer demanded. "It's a Hollywood movie. There'll be press all over it. You know how the Japanese are going to react—"

"It's under control," Alec cut in, even though the venture wasn't anywhere near under control. He was attracted to Charlotte, and he'd let that attraction overrule his logic. Filming a movie in his living room? Kiefer, his vice president, was right to be ticked off. They'd met with a high-priced image consultant only last week, and Alec had agreed to try to be more circumspect in his personal life.

"Kana Hanako wants a business partner, not a playboy."

"It's a business deal," said Alec, taking a swig from his water bottle, refusing to acknowledge Kiefer's point. "They're renting the château."

"Who's the star?"

"Ridley Sinclair."

Kiefer snorted. "You know what I mean."

"Isabella Hudson. I've never even met her."

Kiefer gaped at him. "*The* Isabella Hudson?"

Like there would be another. "She is a member of the family."

"You're going to have Isabella Hudson staying at the Château Montcalm. Good God, Alec, why not just go ahead and murder someone? Even the Japanese tabloids will pick up you and Isabella Hudson."

"I'm not going near Isabella Hudson. There'll be no pictures, nothing whatsoever for them to report."

But Kiefer wasn't listening. He was inside his own

head, obviously dreaming up one dire scenario after another. "You're going to have to move out."

"No," said Alec.

"Go stay in Rome. Better still, go to Tokyo and work with Akiko on the prototype."

"They don't need me in the bike lab." If the one he was riding was anything to go on, R & D had made great strides with the frame alloy.

"Well, I need you out of Provence."

They crested the hill, and Alec grabbed a higher gear, putting his frustration into muscle power that produced speed. Let a film crew invade his house yet *miss* his chance with Charlotte? No way.

"I am staying in my home," he told Kiefer, bending his head into the wind.

"We need a mitigation strategy," Kiefer called, falling slightly behind.

"Mitigate this!" Alec sent back a rude hand gesture.

"Don't let the press catch you doing that." Kiefer caught up. "Could you maybe get married?" he huffed.

Alec rolled his eyes. He'd yet to meet a woman who wasn't after his money or his status—usually both.

"At least find a girlfriend? Not forever, just while Isabella is there. Somebody who's a nobody, a plain Jane who won't get you into any trouble."

Alec didn't want a plain Jane nobody. And he had zero interest in Isabella Hudson. He wanted Charlotte.

And then he realized he'd missed his big chance. "Damn," he spat out.

"What?" Kiefer glanced from side to side.

He could have made that a condition of the movie location deal. What was he thinking? Charlotte could have played his girlfriend for a couple of months.

"What?" Kiefer repeated.

But it was too late now. She didn't strike him as the kind of person who would renegotiate.

"I almost had a girl we could bribe," Alec admitted.

"Who?"

Alec shook his head. "We missed the boat on that one."

"Who is she?"

"Nobody."

"Perfect," said Kiefer with enthusiasm.

"I lost my leverage." Alec slowed his bike, taking a right-hand turn into the pullout beside Crystal Lake.

"Well, what was your leverage?" Kiefer's voice was eager.

"Oh, no, you don't." Alec braked to a halt and put his feet down, taking in the view of the lake while they took a breather.

"Oh, no, I don't what?"

"She's smart, tough and unreasonable."

"At least give me a shot." Kiefer squirted a stream of water into his open mouth.

"There's no real problem," said Alec. "The Kana Hanako brass aren't going to give up my Tour de France connection, no matter what the tabloids write."

"Yeah, but they can make my life hell in the meantime. Do you know how much time I waste being yelled at by Takahiro's translator?"

"Do you know how much I pay you to get yelled at by Takahiro's translator?"

"Not nearly enough," Kiefer grumbled. Then he recapped his water bottle and ran spread fingers through his short hair. "Who were you talking about?"

Alec shook his head.

"I swear I won't even talk to her."

Alec paused. "Charlotte Hudson. She's the friend of Raine's."

"Ah." Kiefer instantly caught on. "You could have bribed her with access to the château."

Alec nodded.

"She's not Isabella's sister or something?"

"Maybe a cousin. I'm not sure. Raine says Charlotte grew up with her maternal grandparents, mostly in Europe. Her grandfather's the U.S. ambassador to Monte Allegro. She works for him."

"Sounds tame enough," Kiefer mused.

"The plan's off the table. I had a hard enough time getting her to stay at the château for the shoot."

Kiefer came alert. "She's staying at the château?"

"Don't touch it." Alec's tone was flat.

"I'm just sayin'—"

"You are *not* leaking her to the press."

"Well, somebody's going to 'leak' something. Better it's her than Isabella."

"In whose opinion?"

"Mine."

"You don't count. You're the hired help." Alec snapped one foot back onto the pedal and pushed off.

Kiefer quickly followed suit. "Will you at least ask her?"

"I will not."

"If she says no, she says no. But she might—"

"She'll never agree."

"How do you know?"

Alec pulled onto the rough road for the return trip. "It's like this," he explained with exaggerated patience. "You're executive assistant to an ambassador. You like your job. In fact, the ambassador is your own grand-father. A man with a public reputation like mine asks you to pretend to date him in order to protect his reputation. You say…what, exactly?"

"Point taken," Kiefer admitted.

They rode in silence to the crest of the hill, where Alec's thoughts turned to the croissants his cook had been putting in the oven when they left the château.

"Still," Kiefer continued, as their speed picked up and the morning air whipped past, "the worst she can do is say no."

"No, no, no," Charlotte emphasized into the cordless telephone. "You *can't* put Syria next to Bulgaria. Put them next to Canada, or the Swiss—"

The telephone handset was summarily tugged out of Charlotte's hand.

"Hey!" She twisted her head to Raine, who was lying back in the next deck lounger.

"Charlotte has to go now, Emily," Raine said into the handset. "She's in the middle of a pedicure."

"You can't do that," Charlotte protested.

But Raine calmly hit the off button.

"You need to hold still," warned the esthetician working on Charlotte's toes. "Or you'll have purple passion streaked halfway to your ankle."

"You listen to her." Raine gestured with the phone.

"You hung up on Emily."

"You've been on the phone with her for half an hour."

"It's the summit dinner. She was about to put Syria next to Bulgaria."

"Will it cause a war?"

"Maybe," said Charlotte, glancing down at her toes.

The purple passion sparkled in the sunshine. She'd borrowed a sea-blue two-piece bathing suit from Raine, and they were lounging on thickly padded lounge chairs next to the Montcalm pool. An emerald lawn stretched out in front of them, while lush cypress trees and flowering shrubs screened them from the house, offering dappled shade.

"They're cultural attachés," Raine pointed out. "I doubt they have the launch codes."

"Maybe not. But I can't just walk away from my responsibilities on a moment's notice." Charlotte had spoken with her grandfather this morning, and he'd been more than gracious in giving her the time off, telling her not to worry. But there were about a thousand details she had to make sure were passed on to other staff members.

"I did," said Raine. "When I heard you were here, I walked right off the shoot in Malta and onto the corporate jet."

"Is that a problem?" Charlotte quickly asked.

"I guess we'll find out when the October issue hits the stands, won't we?"

"No, seriously—"

"The magazine will survive, and so will the ambassador. You need to relax."

"You should not move for at least half an hour," Charlotte's esthetician advised, admiring Charlotte's toes as she rose from her chair.

"Thank you," said Charlotte, raising her newly polished fingernails and fluttering them to compare to her matching toes.

Raine's esthetician finished a final topcoat, and the two women began to pack their things.

Charlotte leaned over to whisper to Raine. "Do we tip or something?"

"All taken care of," Raine whispered back. "Shall I ring for strawberries and champagne?"

"It's still morning."

"You're on vacation. And you're in Provence." Raine grinned and hit a speed-dial button on the phone.

"At this rate, I may never leave," Charlotte muttered, sighing and relaxing back into the soft lounger.

While Raine talked to the kitchen, Charlotte closed her eyes, letting the soft breeze caress her face and listening to the gentle hum of the cicadas fill in the background.

"Quick!" Raine's elbow jolted Charlotte back to reality. "Take a look."

Charlotte blinked against the bright sunshine, scanning the lawn beyond the pool and coming to two male figures.

Alec. And he was dressed in bicycle shorts and a spandex shirt that clung to every sculpted muscle.

"Isn't he the hottest thing you've ever seen?" asked Raine.

He was, but it seemed an odd thing for Raine to notice. "Alec?"

"Nooo." Raine grimaced. "Kiefer. The guy with him."

"Oh." Charlotte hadn't paid the least bit of attention to the slightly shorter man with short, sandy-blond hair striding down the brick pathway next to Alec.

"He's our vice president," Raine elaborated. "The girls in the office go ga-ga over him."

"Sounds like you do, too." Charlotte chuckled, watching the man named Kiefer saunter closer. He was probably six foot two. Though a slighter build than Alec, he was well muscled with an angular face, square jaw and an easy, self-confident stride.

"Don't you dare say a word," Raine warned.

"You don't want to date an employee?" Charlotte asked, her gaze moving involuntarily to Alec. Now *that* was a gorgeous man. Everything about him moved in perfect symmetry.

"I don't want him to think I'm one of his groupies," Raine corrected.

"It's that bad?"

"Just look at him," Raine scoffed.

Charlotte glanced back for a split second. Sure, he was attractive enough. But she wasn't sensing the animal magnetism she saw in Alec. If the girls in the office were going to go ga-ga, she would have thought Alec would be their target.

The two women halted their conversation as the men came within earshot. They stopped in front of the two loungers. Kiefer's gaze swept Charlotte without sparing a single glance for Raine.

"*This* is your plain Jane?" Kiefer asked Alec, astonishment clear in his tone.

Charlotte shot Alec an exaggerated expression of offense. "I'm your *what?*"

Alec's jaw tightened. "Smooth, Kiefer." He drew a breath. "Charlotte, this is my vice president, Kiefer Knight. He's just come up with the most ridiculous idea in the world."

Three

Kiefer pulled a deck chair up next to Charlotte's lounger, angling away from Raine. She could feel Alec's gaze on her honey-brown skin. Maybe a bikini hadn't been such a good idea after all. His attention was raising goose bumps, and she couldn't help imagining his fingers trailing over her stomach, down the length of her legs…

"I'm concerned about Alec's reputation," Kiefer began in a gentle, cajoling voice.

Charlotte forced herself to concentrate on Kiefer's words.

"I understand Isabella Hudson is starring in your movie."

"My family's movie," Charlotte corrected. All she'd done was secure the location. Well, and she was going to babysit the shoot. But that was only because Alec was being obstinate. She really had no role here except pandering to his need for power and control.

"If they're together here, rumors about Alec and Isabella are bound to circulate."

Her gaze shifted to Alec, who still stood indolently at the foot of her lounger, taking in the color of her toenails.

"You're involved with Bella?" she asked him. For some reason, the idea put a cramp in her belly.

"You're botching this," Alec growled at Kiefer.

Kiefer held up his hands in surrender. "Be my guest."

"Kiefer wants you to pretend to be my girlfriend to forestall any gossip about me and Isabella."

Charlotte tried to sort out his words. "You're dating Bella?" Why hadn't Isabella asked for the use of the château? Why had Jack sent Charlotte? And what was Alec doing flirting with *her?*

"I am *not* dating Isabella," he huffed in exasperation.

"But she's high profile," Kiefer put in. "And beautiful. And the press will invent their own headlines."

Charlotte got the picture. They wanted to throw her to the wolves to save Alec's reputation. Like there was any hope for Alec's reputation.

"Is this a joke?" she asked.

"Sadly," said Alec, "Kiefer is completely serious."

"He's been gracious enough to let you use the château," Kiefer put in.

"Here's a thought," suggested Charlotte, an edge to her tone. "Alec can keep his hands off Isabella, and then there'll be no reason for a ruse with 'Plain Jane.'"

"I am not going to have my hands *on* Isabella," Alec practically shouted.

Charlotte barely glanced at him then turned to Kiefer. "Problem solved."

"The tabloids don't rely on the truth," said Kiefer.

"Apparently," Charlotte shot back, "neither do you."

"Has anyone thought about Charlotte's reputation?" asked Raine.

"Charlotte has," said Charlotte.

"He could have made it a condition of the contract," Kiefer pointed out.

"He didn't," Alec said flatly.

Charlotte turned to Alec once more. "Do *you* think it's a good idea?" Not that she'd go along with it in any event. And thank goodness Alec hadn't asked for it before they closed the deal.

"I think it's an idea," he said, obviously choosing his words carefully. "Good? Not sure. But it might deflect speculation."

"Since when have you cared about speculation on your love life?"

Kiefer jumped in again. "Since the president of Kana Hanako, our Japanese partner, expressed concern."

"Something I should know about?" asked Raine, her alert, businesslike tone at odds with her bikini-clad pose on the lounger.

Kiefer's attention went to her for the briefest of seconds, but then he blinked and focused on the small pool house behind her. "It's not that serious."

"Then why are we having this conversation? Charlotte's not going to trash her reputation by being seen with Alec—"

"Hello?" Alec tossed in.

Raine waved a dismissive hand. "You made your bed a long time ago, *mon frère*."

"Just don't make a bed with Isabella," Charlotte advised.

"I have *no interest* in Isabella." His eyes darkened to walnut, pinning Charlotte in place. "Can I talk to you in private?"

Not when he looked like that. Not when the predatory set of his jaw made her skin tingle and her spine turn to jelly. "I'm letting my toenails dry."

Both Raine and Kiefer stilled, while Alec stared at her in silence. Clearly, people didn't normally turn down Alec's requests.

"Later, then," he finally said with a tense nod, turning on his heel.

Later proved hard to come by for Alec. Raine and Charlotte took a shopping trip into Toulouse. The location manager, set designer and second-unit director all arrived, followed quickly by carpenters, set dressers and lighting technicians.

The main floor of Alec's house quickly turned into a construction zone. There was more than one moment when he contemplated moving out for the duration. But then he'd catch a glimpse of Charlotte.

The more he saw of her, the more determined he was to get to know her better—much, much better.

He finally caught her alone, leaning on the rail of the third-floor hallway, staring down to the rotunda foyer where the grips were setting tracks for a camera.

"Bonjour," he opened, resting his forearms on the polished wood, matching her pose.

She glanced over at him, then her gaze darted worriedly from the staircase to the front door and to either side of them.

"No photographers," he assured her.

"I don't trust Kiefer," she responded.

"My apologies," Alec offered. "I shouldn't have let him make that request."

"That I fake being your girlfriend?" she clarified.

Alec nodded. Though his only true regret was that she'd said no. It would have given him a perfect excuse to spend time with her. It was also regrettable that the experience had left her suspicious and jumpy. "I promise he won't jump out of the bushes with a camera."

"How do I know I can trust you?"

A piece of equipment crashed in the foyer below. The noise was followed by an exchange of shouts.

"How do I know you won't destroy my home?" Alec countered. "I guess we're both taking a leap of faith."

She turned her head to gaze at him, and he was struck once again by her beauty. Her crystal-blue eyes sparkled in the sunshine that streamed through the stained-glass dome ceiling. Her lips were deep red as they curved up in a wry smile. And her cheeks were rosy highlights to her creamy skin.

"You can rebuild the château," she told him.

"That's three-hundred-year-old limestone on the floor."

Her glance was drawn downward. "So, it must be pretty much indestructible," she offered in a perky voice.

Alec couldn't help but chuckle. "I'm not going to harm your reputation," he promised.

She gave a small nod. "Thank you."

But then a camera flash went off below, and Alec quickly grasped her hand, tugging her through the open door behind them and swiftly closing it against the world.

"Reference shots for the crew back home," she explained, a grin growing on her face. "But thanks for the effort."

"I didn't want to break my word within the first two minutes."

Their hands were still joined as they stood next to the arched, oak-plank door of the third-floor library. Shelves were lined with leather volumes and heavy, green-velvet drapes were pulled aside with gold cording, letting a beam of morning sunshine stream through paned windows. The room was slightly dusky, cool, quiet and still.

Her small hand was soft under his, the skin of her palm warm, hinting at the texture of other regions of her body. He inhaled the clean floral scent of her shampoo. It reminded him of the lavender plants blowing softly in his country garden.

Everything about Charlotte was sweet and fresh, from her white flash of a smile, to the breezy, shoulder-length style of her blond hair. Her figure was lithe and streamlined. He'd watched her play tennis with Raine yesterday, and he knew she was in fabulous shape.

His thoughts trailed back to the way she'd looked by the pool. The aqua bikini had revealed a light, glowing tan. Her belly was flat, with the sexiest navel he'd ever seen. Her shoulders were kissable, and the curve of her breasts had invaded his dreams every night since.

"Alec?" Her voice was soft, in keeping with the atmosphere of the room.

He tugged gently on her hand, drawing her toward him. His gaze fixed on her full lips. "Tell me you haven't been curious," he whispered.

"I—" But then she stopped, her gaze fixed on his lips, apparently unable to lie but unwilling to be honest.

He smiled. "Me, too."

"We can't do this," she warned.

"We're not *doing* anything."

"Oh, yes, we are."

He tugged her closer still, so that she brushed up against him. "At the moment, we're merely talking."

"We're talking about kissing."

"Nothing wrong with kissing."

"You got a camera in your pocket?"

"That's not a camera."

She scrunched her eyes shut. "I can't believe you said that."

"I can't believe it shocked you." He chuckled low. "You're blushing." For some reason, he found her reaction completely endearing.

"I'm embarrassed because the joke was so bad."

"You're embarrassed because you're attracted to me and, for some reason, you think you should fight it."

"Of course I should fight it."

"Why?"

"You're a playboy and a philanderer."

"You say that like it's a bad thing."

"You'll destroy my reputation."

"By kissing you in private? I'm flattered you think I have that kind of power." He drew a breath and held her with a frank gaze. "Charlotte, kiss me, don't kiss me. But at least be honest. Your reputation is in absolutely no danger at the moment."

Her shoulders dropped. "You're right," she admitted.

But she didn't make a move.

It was more than tempting to wrap his arms around her, dip his head and take her lips to his. But he held back. She was still jumpy, and the last thing he wanted to do was scare her off.

He wanted this kiss. Of course, he wanted more than just a kiss, but at least a kiss was heading in the right direction.

To his surprise, she placed a hand on his shoulder.

"It's mere curiosity," she warned.

A half smile crept out. "But of course."

She pulled up on her toes. "I might not even like it."

"You might not," he agreed, holding himself still by sheer force of will.

This time, it was Charlotte who smiled. "Do many women not like kissing you?"

"I can't recall any specific complaints. But I've sure never had one give it this much thought beforehand."

"I'm a planner."

"Evidently."

They both sobered, staring at each other in silence.

"Oh, man." Charlotte moaned a surrender, closing her eyes and stretching up toward him.

It was all the invitation Alec needed.

He immediately leaned in, parting his lips, pressing them to her heated mouth.

An explosion went off at the base of his brain, obliterating everything but the taste, scent and feel of Charlotte. He deepened the kiss, flattening her against the oak door, pressing his body flush against hers.

His hands cupped her face, caressing her skin while holding her in place as his tongue plundered shamelessly. She moaned, opened her mouth wider, and her arms wrapped around his waist. He pushed his thigh between her legs, lifting, bunching her short skirt, the fabric of his slacks meeting the satin of her panties.

His body flushed hot, tense, rigid with desire, and

a freight train roared in his ears and the world contracted to the two of them.

"Charlotte?" came a faraway voice.

Raine.

Charlotte tensed, and Alec groaned, reluctantly taking his mouth from hers. He eased back, knowing they might have only seconds before Raine tried the door.

"Charlotte?" Raine repeated.

"Let go," Charlotte whispered.

Alec took a step back, rasping deep breaths, trying vainly to put his raging hormones back under control.

"You okay?" he asked.

"Fine," Charlotte shot back, smoothing her pleated, navy skirt and straightening the white, sleeveless blouse.

He reached out to fix her mussed hair, and she drew in a sharp breath. There was nothing he could do about the just-kissed puffiness of her mouth—except try like hell not to get turned on by it.

The doorknob rattled, and Charlotte jumped back. "Why are we in here?" she frantically whispered.

Alec drew open the door. "Raine?" He gazed at the quizzical expression on his sister's face. "I'm glad it's you," he continued. "There was a photographer downstairs, and Charlotte got a little freaked out." He gave Charlotte a teasing wink. "I told her there was nothing to worry about. Did you see anyone skulking around with a camera?"

Rained glanced at Charlotte, then back to Alec. "No."

"Good," he said heartily. "I'll be in my office. Kiefer should be here in an hour or so. If you see him, could you have Henri send him straight up?"

With Raine suitably distracted by erroneous details,

and having given Charlotte at least a couple of minutes to recover, Alec exited the room.

Then, three steps down the hallway, he put a hand against the wall to steady himself. It was a kiss, he reminded himself, a simple kiss.

Except that it hadn't been simple. It had blown his expectations right out of the water. If he'd been attracted to Charlotte before, he was nearly wild for her now. The chemistry between them was nothing short of mind-blowing, and he wasn't going to be able to focus on Kana Hanako or anything else until he investigated it further.

"I don't blame you for being paranoid," said Raine, as Alec left the library.

"Hmm?" Charlotte stalled, not yet capable of producing actual words. Her skin was tingling, her heart was thumping and her knees felt as if they'd been turned to gelatin.

"Kiefer can be devious."

"Right." Charlotte nodded, telling herself to snap out of it. The kiss had been good—well, great, actually. But she'd expected it to be great. If she hadn't, she wouldn't have bothered kissing Alec, would she? What woman would embark on a kiss she thought would be boring?

"One picture of you and Alec, doing something as innocent as having a conversation, and Kiefer gets his nefarious wish. You want me to talk to him?" Raine paused. "Charlotte?"

"What?"

"You want me to talk to Kiefer? Or maybe you should steer clear of Alec. Just to be on the safe side."

Charlotte drew a deep breath and gave herself a

mental shake. "Yeah. Good idea." Steering clear of Alec was better than the alternative—hauling him into the nearest bed and kissing him until her brain exploded.

"Mademoiselle Charlotte?" came a new voice from the hallway. Henri.

Raine turned to meet him. "*Oui*, Henri?"

"A Jack Hudson has arrived."

"Jack's here?" The words jumped from Charlotte as a familiar little knot grew in her stomach. She loved her big brother. But their relationship was complicated.

She couldn't help remembering Alec and Raine's greeting embrace. Charlotte hadn't hugged Jack in more than twenty years—not since she'd been torn from his arms in the airport at four years old, after her mother died, after her own father gave her away.

The next time they'd seen each other, he'd felt like a stranger. She wasn't sure how to act, and neither was he.

He didn't seem like the strong, protective big brother she'd fantasized about at night. Their visits grew further apart, and the awkwardness became acute in their teenage years. And now, as adults, neither seemed to know how to break the barrier.

Or maybe Jack didn't want to break the barrier. He was a grown man with his own life. Why would he need a little sister hanging all over him?

She squared her shoulders and headed to the hallway. Once she got through the initial hello, it was always easier.

Raine fell into step beside her. "You okay?"

"I'm fine."

"You look a little pale."

Better pale with anxiety than flushed with sexual desire, Charlotte supposed.

"Everything's moving smoothly," Raine offered. She knew of Charlotte's desire to impress the Hudson side of the family. "Even Lars Hinckleman is happy today."

Charlotte couldn't help but smile at the mention of the temperamental second-unit director. Raine was right. Things were going—

"I said *dramatic,* not *appalling!*" Lars shouted from the bottom of the stairs.

"Spoke too soon," Raine muttered, as Charlotte quickened her steps on the curved, wrought-iron-railed staircase.

The stocky man was waving his arms, an unlit cigar clamped between his teeth, his dark hair curling over his forehead.

"It's authentic Stix, Baer & Fuller," the costume assistant dared, causing the entire room to hush and collectively suck in a breath.

Even Charlotte missed a step. Lars had been at the château for only three days, but she'd quickly learned the near-military command-control structure of the film set.

Lars leaned into the hapless young woman, his dark, round eyes narrowing. "Lillian Hudson will *not* wear a bird's nest on her head."

"She was Lillian Colbert then."

The man's face turned purple.

The costume designer quickly stepped in. "We'll come up with other options, of course." She latched on to the younger woman's arm and deftly drew her away.

"Fire that thing," Lars huffed to an assistant.

The assistant made a note on a clipboard and said something into his walkie-talkie. Charlotte fervently hoped the command was all bluster. Then she spotted Jack.

He was talking to the director of photography, ignoring the commotion on set, while everyone around him continued with set preparation.

"That's your brother?" asked Raine.

Charlotte nodded, putting one foot in front of the other as she made her way across the foyer.

"You look alike."

Charlotte disagreed. Jack was much darker. He was dignified, where she was decidedly cute. "No, we don't."

"It's your nose, and the eyes," said Raine. "That vivid blue. Gorgeous."

Charlotte gazed at Jack as they drew near. Did they look alike? Did people notice? Could there be other things they had in common? Thoughts, opinions, emotions?

"Hello, Charlotte." He greeted her with a broad smile.

"Good morning, Jack." As always, she felt like there was something she should do. A hug? A kiss? A handshake?

He glanced around the huge rotunda. "Well done," he told her, sounding sincere.

At least she had that. "This is Raine Montcalm," she introduced.

The director of photography was drawn into another conversation and turned away.

Jack reached out to shake Raine's hand. "On behalf of the family, allow me to express our gratitude for opening up your home."

A brief pain shot through Charlotte's chest. Clearly, Jack didn't see her as a representative of the Hudsons. She'd already thanked the Montcalms, but that obviously wasn't good enough.

"Alec Montcalm." Alec's deep voice startled Charlotte.

He moved up beside her and shook Jack's hand.

"Jack Hudson." Jack introduced himself before she could get her bearings. "My grandmother sends her thanks."

Alec's fingertips touched ever so lightly on the small of Charlotte's back. "You sister made a convincing argument."

Jack smiled down at Charlotte. "We were hoping her connection to Raine would help."

Alec's hand tensed almost imperceptibly. "Yes. Well, I hope you're happy with the results."

"We'll also need a couple of rental houses for the VIPs and stars," said Jack. "Any suggestions?"

"I can make a couple of calls."

"I don't want to put you to any trouble."

"No trouble," said Alec. "Charlotte?" He glanced down, his palm warm on her back. "Maybe you could give me a hand?"

More time with Alec?

Her mind screamed no. While her body shouted yes. Then her reflexive nod broke the tie.

To her surprise, instead of taking her back to his office for privacy, he said goodbyes and ushered her out the front door.

"I thought we were making a few calls?" she said as Alec cut toward the garage. She scrambled to keep up in her heels. The sunshine was warm on her bare arms and legs, and the sweet smell of the estate's flowers and herb gardens invaded her nostrils.

"I brought my cell," said Alec.

"Where are we going?"

He hit the button on a small remote and one of the garage doors glided open, revealing a burnished copper Lamborghini convertible. The top was down, showing off a black and copper interior, a sexy console and low-slung leather bucket seats.

"Nice," she acknowledged.

"Thanks." He popped open the passenger door then offered a hand to steady her as she climbed in.

"Where are we going?" she repeated, even as her body all but sighed into the soft leather. It would be nice to get away from the chaos for a while, clear her head, remember there were other things in life besides the approval of the Hudsons.

In answer to her question, Alec grinned and gestured to the sky. "A day like this? In the south of France? In a Murciélago? Who cares?"

He made a good point.

Charlotte shrugged both in agreement and capitulation. The seat surrounded her body like a glove. Alec leaned in, pulled out the seat belt and reached across to click it into the buckle. She couldn't resist inhaling his scent, fresh and clean like the region where he lived.

He shut the door, then rounded the hood to the driver's side, removing his jacket and rolling up the sleeves of his white dress shirt. Next, he untied his tie, slipping it off and setting it behind the seat.

Charlotte glanced around at the classy interior. She couldn't help a smile at the thought of zooming through the countryside in such a magnificent vehicle.

Henri magically appeared and retrieved the jacket. "You have everything you need, sir?"

Alec nodded, perching a pair of sunglasses on his nose.

"You ready?" he asked Charlotte.

"I don't have my purse," she remembered.

"Sir?" asked Henri.

"She won't need it," said Alec, turning the key. The powerful engine roared to life, rumbling the seat beneath her. He clicked the car into gear and pulled smoothly out of the garage. They passed semitrailers containing warehouses of filming equipment, one that was a wardrobe room, and another containing a full, industrial kitchen.

"I thought you might like to get away from the circus for a while," said Alec, picking up speed down the long, concrete driveway.

"That Lars makes me nervous."

"I don't know why people put up with him."

"I guess he's in charge for the moment." The second-unit filming was scheduled to take place before the stars and director arrived.

The car came to a smooth stop at the end of the driveway, and Alec turned it toward Castres.

"Being in charge is no excuse for being a jerk."

"Not an excuse," Charlotte agreed. "But it's a reason."

"There's never a reason to abuse power," said Alec, bringing up the revs and changing gears as the road straightened out.

Charlotte considered his profile for a moment.

He glanced over. "What?"

"You have power," she observed, wondering what he was like with his own employees, remembering how he'd insisted the film crew not cause them any additional work.

"At the moment." He winked, gearing down and pulling into the oncoming lane to pass a truck. "I also have speed."

The sports car stuck to the road like glue, accelerating effortlessly past the truck and another car in front.

Charlotte's hand automatically gripped the door handle.

"Nervous?" asked Alec.

"Not exactly." There was something about Alec that oozed confidence behind the wheel. Well, actually, there was something about him that oozed confidence about *everything*. She trusted him not to push himself or the car past their limits.

"I won't hurt you," he assured her in a solemn tone.

She'd have to be blind not to catch the double entendre. "How can you be sure?"

"With power comes responsibility," he said, easing back into the proper lane. "I was born to both."

Did she dare trust him with her sexual attraction? And was that what this was about? Was he whisking her off to some discreet inn where they could spend the afternoon in bed exploring it?

Pretty bold of him not to ask her. She should tell him no. Just to thwart his arrogant self-confidence, she should tell him she wasn't interested in a tryst.

He flipped on his signal and left the main road.

And maybe she would.

Soon.

In the meantime, she watched the businesses roll by on the tree-lined boulevard, keeping an eye out for possible hotels and inns. They passed one, then another, then a small bed-and-breakfast.

But, to her surprise, Alec pulled into the parking lot of a real-estate office.

She raised her brows. "Here?"

"My friend Renaldo," said Alec. "He'll let us know what's up for rent."

"Oh." Didn't Charlotte feel like a fool. "A real-estate office."

A knowing light came into Alec's eyes. "What were you expecting?"

"This," she quickly responded with a nod.

He grinned, and she felt her face heat.

Four

Alec wanted to sleep with Charlotte—so much so that it was beginning to feel like an obsession. That kiss this morning told him they would all but combust together, and the confused looks she'd been giving him said she'd felt it, too. And now they were alone. They had several hours to spend together. And there were endless possible locations to make love in town. They had everything but a set of runway lights guiding them to paradise.

But something was holding him back. And he couldn't begin to imagine what it might be. Guys like him could talk women into bed without breaking a sweat. Half the time it was about his money, of course. But then half the time he didn't really care.

Maybe he was getting old. Or maybe he wanted to

pretend it was different with Charlotte—that there was more to it than sex on his side and manipulation on hers.

Which didn't make sense. He barely knew her. She could be as susceptible to his millions as every other woman he'd met in this lifetime. Just because she was Raine's friend, and just because she was bright and witty, with an endearing dash of vulnerability, didn't make her any different from anyone else.

Still, instead of rushing her to the nearest hotel room, he found himself winding his way through Castres to the first of three houses available for rent.

The first one was an old, converted mill set next to the river on a few acres of lawn.

"Gorgeous," sang Charlotte, tipping her head back and turning in a circle as they entered a boxy, high-ceilinged main room. A polished wooden staircase was set against the stone wall and led up to the landing on the second story. The wood floors gleamed, and the furniture was big and comfortable.

"You think it might be too small?" asked Alec.

"It's charming," said Charlotte, passing beneath the staircase, past the stone fireplace to the arched doorway that led to a restored kitchen. Bright enamel pots hung from the ceiling, and a giant white sink dominated the counter below a window that looked out over the water. The cupboards were worn, and the floor tiles had definitely seen better days.

Alec tested the table for dust. "We're talking about bigwigs and movie stars."

Charlotte frowned at him. "I'd stay here," she declared, wandering to the big sink.

He followed. "Yeah? Well, apparently, you're not all that fussy."

She turned suddenly, and they were nearly nose to nose, her back trapped against the sink.

"How would you know that?" she asked.

He held up his finger to show the dust, rubbing it off with his thumb.

She watched the motion, and he felt a flicker of warning heat build up inside him.

"Nothing a little elbow grease won't fix," she said.

"I'm guessing stars don't do windows," he countered, attempting to keep the mood light.

"Of course not. They have people who do it for them. But then, you'd know all about that, wouldn't you?"

"Got a problem with my money?" Sarcasm wasn't the female reaction he normally experienced.

She paused. "I like your car."

"You have good taste."

"You like to go fast?"

He digested the statement for a second, wondering which tack to take.

A flicker of unease crossed her face.

"I like to go fast," he agreed softly, keeping his expression steady, allowing her decide whether to let it drop or pick it up and run with it.

They stared at each other in silence. The river rushed by below the window, and a songbird serenaded them from a nearby tree branch. The house itself was still and silent. It seemed to be holding its breath along with them.

"I thought the kiss would get us out of this," she finally said.

"I guess it didn't," he responded.

Another minute went by.

"Shouldn't you be doing something?" she asked.

"Like what?"

"I don't know, something decisive one way or the other."

He smiled. "I thought about that. And then I thought I'd let you make the first move."

She shifted against the cool ceramic sink. "And if I don't?"

He shrugged. "Then I guess it's like a staring contest. We'll see who blinks first."

"And you think that would be fun?"

"I think it would be fascinating." And he did.

He had a will of iron when he wanted it. Not that he necessarily wanted it in this case. But toying with Charlotte was like stomping the accelerator of his Lamborghini. It was always exhilarating to see which would come first, disaster or delirium.

"In that case." She slipped sideways, dancing away from him, across the kitchen. "I'm betting I can hold out longer than you."

"You think?"

She snagged his attention with a sultry, sexy look. "I guess we'll find out. Where's the next house?"

"Rue du Blanc. Top of the hill."

It was a modern stone villa with twelve rooms and a pool overlooking an olive grove. Charlotte liked it. So did Alec. The kitchen was clean and modern, and there were plenty of bedrooms and enough baths for an entourage.

Their final stop was a full-on castle, with bleached stones, hewn ceiling beams, a formal dining room and seven bedrooms with king-size beds. A gilded fountain dominated the driveway turnaround, while acres of emerald lawn stretched out front. The furniture was

French provincial, with many valuable antiques dotting the impressively large rooms. Out back, there was a swimming pool and a meticulously maintained garden maze that was a work of art.

"I hope they're not a party crowd," Alec observed as they moved from the patio back into the formal dining room. Too many highballs, and somebody was going to get hopelessly lost in that maze.

"Okay, now I envy your money," said Charlotte, making her way back to the grand entrance hall with its octagonal windows, antique rugs and tapestry. "I'd love to pick up something like this on a whim."

"You like it that much?" asked Alec.

She nodded. "I'd buy it."

"The kitchen's a little small."

"I'd renovate."

He chuckled. "You'd actually knock out a stone wall?"

She flung open the double doors to the great room. "It's my fantasy," she pointed out, walking through the furniture groupings, past oil portraits and a massive, rolltop desk. "I guess I can knock out whatever I want."

At the far end of the great room, there was a balcony overlooking a duck pond. Charlotte wandered into the sunshine and leaned on the wide rail. "If I lived here, I could name the ducks."

"You could," he agreed, moving next to her. "Though I'm not sure how you'd tell them apart."

"I'd buy a dog. Put up a swing for the kids."

"Kids?"

"Sure. I wouldn't use all seven bedrooms myself." A wistful expression came over her face as she gazed into the distance, obviously imagining a picture-perfect family.

"So, what's with you and Jack?" Alec ventured, reminded of her real family.

She kept her eyes straight forward. "What do you mean?"

Alec had seen the expression on her face. He'd watched their body language, and the distance they kept between them. "It seemed like there was some kind of tension—"

"I don't know what you're talking about."

"Are you angry with him?" It seemed like the most logical explanation.

"Why would I be angry with him?"

"I don't know. It was—"

"I barely know him."

Alec took in her profile for a moment. "He's your brother."

"We didn't grow up together."

Alec had heard as much from Raine. "What happened?"

She brushed a speck of sand off the concrete rail, then scratched her thumbnail over a flaw. "When I was four, my mother died. Jack stayed with the Hudson grandparents, and I went with the Cassettes."

Alec found his heart going out to her. His parents had died when he was in his twenties, and that was enough of a blow. And he'd always had Raine. Charlotte, on the other hand, had her entire family ripped away when she was little more than a baby. No wonder she fantasized about home and hearth.

"Did you ever ask why?"

"Ask Jack?"

"Your father."

She shook her head. "David Hudson and I don't talk much."

Alec stilled her small hand with his own. "I guess not."

She shrugged her slim, bare shoulders. "It was hardly *Oliver Twist*."

"But it hurt you just the same."

She smoothed back her hair, raking spread fingers through the tangles. "It's just...sometimes..." But then she shook her head.

"Tell me," he prompted.

She turned to look at him. "Like you and Raine. You hug, you tease." She moved her hands in a gesture of confusion.

"That comes from years of learning exactly how to push each other's buttons."

"That might be how you tease her, but that's not why you hug her."

Suddenly, Charlotte looked so vulnerable and confused and alone on the windswept balcony that he couldn't help himself. He wrapped his arms around her and drew her against him, cradling her head against his shoulder and smoothing her tousled hair.

"Be patient," he advised. "Relationships are complicated."

"I'm twenty-five," said Charlotte. "And we live on different continents."

"Some are more complicated than others."

Her body trembled against his.

"Hey," he soothed, rubbing his palm across her back, trying desperately to keep his perspective. But she was soft and sexy in his arms. She smelled like a spring garden, and the vivid memory of her taste was pounding inside his head.

She drew back, and he was surprised to see she was laughing instead of crying.

"What's funny?" he asked.

"I guess Jack and I would be on the complicated end of the spectrum."

Alec gazed into her bright eyes, her flushed cheeks, the wild hair begging to be smoothed out of the way.

"No." He shook his head, and she sobered under his expression. "You and *I* would be on the complicated end of the spectrum." And he bent his head to kiss her tempting lips.

The instant Alec's lips touched hers, Charlotte knew how he did it. She knew why dozens if not hundreds of women fell head over heels for him, knew why they clambered into his bed and made fools of themselves in public.

He wasn't just gorgeous, wasn't just sexy, wasn't just a rich man who could wine them and dine them all over the planet. Alec Montcalm was magic.

It was in his eyes, in his touch, in his voice that made a woman feel like she was the only person on earth.

Her arms wound around his neck, and she tipped her head to better accommodate his kiss. His hot lips parted, and she invited him in, parrying with his tongue while his arms tightened. Her breasts pressed against his chest, and she could feel a tingle start within her nipples, radiating out to touch every fiber of her being.

He whispered her name, then kissed her deeper, backing her against the rail. His hands cradled her face, thumbs stroking her cheeks, fingertips burying in her hairline. It was, hands down, the most sensual kiss she'd ever experienced.

Their bodies were plastered together, and his lips began to roam. First to her cheek, her temple, her eyelids. Then he kissed the lobe of her ear, making his way down the curve of her neck.

She struggled to breathe, her lips still tingling. Her hands found his short hair, tunneling their way through its coarse softness. His kisses found her mouth again, and she moaned her appreciation.

Her clothes suddenly felt stifling, and the waning sun was hot on her back. Sweat prickled her skin and she longed to tear off her clothes to get some respite from the suddenly humid air.

Then he clasped her to him, lifting her right off the patio, turning, breathing deeply in her ear.

"We have to stop," he rasped, even as she kissed his salty neck.

She wasn't sure why, so she kept right on kissing.

"Not here," he elaborated with obvious strain.

Of course.

Not here.

They were in a stranger's house.

What was she thinking?

She stopped kissing, burying her face against his shoulder. His skin was superheated, the cotton of his shirt damp against her cheek.

"Sorry," she managed between breaths.

"Hell, I'm sure not."

"We can't keep doing this." She was warning herself as much as she was warning him. If they kept it up, sooner or later, they were going to make love, even if they didn't find the perfect time and location.

"We can," he argued. "But sooner or later, we'll get caught."

"The tabloids," she confirmed, appreciating his concern for her reputation.

"I was thinking of your brother," Alec admitted, still holding her tight. "But, yes, let's go with the tabloids."

"There's only one of Jack," Charlotte noted, not exactly sure of her point. What was she suggesting?

"You saying we can outsmart him?"

"I'm saying he can't be everywhere." She paused. "But the tabloids can." And they were definitely worth worrying about.

"So, what do we do?"

"You might want to put me down."

He gently loosened his arms, letting her slide sensually along his body until her shoes met the deck.

"Damn it," he gasped.

Passion ricocheted along her nerve endings, and she silently echoed his curse. She forced herself to take a step back, and he let her go.

She laughed weakly, turning her attention to the fields, the duck pond and the distant orchard, struggling valiantly to bring her emotions under control. "You do have a way with women, Alec."

He was silent for a long moment, and when he spoke there was a distance in his tone. "Not all women."

Maybe not. But she was willing to bet it was with most women. "We need to get back," she managed.

"Of course," he agreed.

Then he waited for her to start back through the great room. He followed more slowly, locking up behind them.

In the Lamborghini, Charlotte tipped her head back and closed her eyes, letting the wind buffet her senses while Alec sped back to Château Montcalm and normal life.

There was nothing remotely normal about Alec's world. He'd expected a disruption in the château, but nothing had prepared him for five semitrailers in the front yard, a hundred crew members, several dozen extras, one temperamental second-unit director and two demanding stars.

The worst part was, his very reason for doing this, Charlotte, had all but disappeared. Claiming Alec had monopolized too much of Charlotte's time when they checked out the rental houses, Raine had latched on to her and stuck by her side round the clock. Not that Alec begrudged them their tennis and spa visits, but was a few minutes alone with Charlotte so much to ask? Sure, they had breakfast and dinner together, but Raine was always there, and sometimes Kiefer, Jack or even Lars joined them.

Suddenly, there was yet another crash in the front yard, followed by shouts and the booming voice of Lars. Alec stood up, crossed the room and pulled his office window shut, securing the latch. The barrier dampened the noise, and he breathed a sigh of relief. Then he settled back into his desk to review the marketing strategy Kana Hanako was proposing leading up to the Tour de France.

So far, none of the tabloids had made a link between Alec and Isabella, even though she'd arrived in Provence two days ago. She and costar Ridley Sinclair had chosen the modern villa in the olive grove, and were sharing it along with a few entourage members.

The growl of a motor buzzed its way through the wall. It grew louder and louder, actually shaking the foundation of the château.

Alec threw down his pen, jerked to his feet and stomped his way through the hallways to the entry, ducking under booms and avoiding cameras and light stands as he made his way to his front door.

He cut through the open doorway in time to see a massive, truck-mounted crane come to a halt on his driveway turnaround. Huge, hydraulic arms whined out to smack into the ground, stabilizing the unit. The key grip shouted directions to the crane operator.

"What the hell?" Alec asked to no one in particular.

"An aerial shot of the balcony scene," a crew member offered.

Just then, the crane shifted. One of the arms broke the concrete with a deafening boom, and the ground shook.

A few people shrieked, but then most settled to laughing nervously as the disturbance subsided.

Alec wasn't laughing. His driveway was ruined.

"Where is Charlotte?" he growled. This was her job. She'd promised to keep the film crew from destroying his home.

"Where is Charlotte?" he asked in a louder voice.

The three closest crew members turned to look at him.

"I want to speak to Charlotte Hudson," he enunciated.

One of the crew members spoke into his walkie-talkie.

"Alec?" came Raine's voice.

He turned to find the two women, small souvenir bags

in tow, jaunty hats on their heads and pretty tans on their perky faces.

"Where the hell have you been?" he demanded, making a beeline to Charlotte.

Her eyes widened. She opened her mouth, but no sound came out.

"This was *your* job," he shouted, gesturing at the chaos around him. "We might as well be having an earthquake. The château is shaking off its foundation. The driveway is destroyed. And I can't even hear myself think."

"I'll—"

"I want that crane gone," he roared. "And I want it gone *now*." He caught Jack in his peripheral vision.

"But—"

"And no more sightseeing. No more spas. No more fun and games with Raine while I suffer this noise and destruction alone." He was ranting now, but he couldn't seem to stop himself. All he'd asked was that she hang around and make sure these people didn't ruin his life. Even that seemed to be too much trouble.

"They need the crane shot," she tried, but her mouth was pinched and her skin was going pale under the tan.

"And I need my château to be standing when this is all over."

She shrank back, and Alec could have kicked himself.

Instead, he turned on Jack. "And *you?* What the hell's the matter with you? I'm standing here screaming at your sister."

Jack blinked in obvious confusion.

"Why don't you hit me?"

Now everybody within earshot looked confused.

Alec cursed under his breath, stomping back into the château, thinking seriously about an extended trip to Rome until this was all over.

* * *

Charlotte stared at her brother, but his gaze slid away, and he became instantly interested in a list on one of the production assistants' clipboards. The noise level in the immediate area went back to normal, as everyone's attention went to their jobs.

Raine shifted toward Charlotte. "That's not normal," she intoned.

"Thank goodness," said Charlotte.

"I don't know what got into him."

"He's not wrong," said Charlotte. "I did promise to make sure everything ran smoothly."

"Alec doesn't yell," said Raine. "He stews. He plots. He might methodically bankrupt you. But he doesn't yell."

"So, I've pushed him over the edge." Charlotte needed to go clear the air. She couldn't leave things hanging between them like this. She subconsciously started toward the front door.

"It appears you have," Raine mused, giving Charlotte a considering look as she fell into step beside her. "Is there something you're not telling me?"

"Like what?" Charlotte stalled, not wanting to lie to her friend, but *really* not wanting to admit she was attracted to Alec. It was so cliché, so tiresome.

"Like maybe he made a pass at you? And you turned him down. Alec's not used to hearing the word no."

"I guess not," Charlotte chuckled.

"So, did he?" asked Raine, keeping her voice low. "Make a pass at me?"

Raine elbowed her in the ribs. "Are you avoiding the question?"

"Pretty much."

"He *did*." Raine linked her arm with Charlotte, steering her down the walkway, through a wooden gate and into a secluded garden where they sat down at a white-painted, wrought-iron table next to a trickling fountain. "So, you said no?" There was a fiendish glee in Raine's wide grin.

"Not exactly," Charlotte admitted, setting down her purse and the small bag.

Her friend's eyes went wide. "You said *yes?*"

"I didn't really say anything."

"Oh my God. You two—"

"No!" Then Charlotte lowered her voice. "No. We didn't."

"I don't understand."

"We kissed." Charlotte sat back in the straight-backed chair. "We kissed, okay?"

"So, why's he mad at you?"

"I'm guessing it's because the crane broke your driveway."

Raine toyed with a tiny leaf that had blown onto the grid-work table. "Trust me when I tell you Alec doesn't yell over broken driveways. And what was that thing with Jack hitting him?"

"You got me," said Charlotte, more than happy to move off the kiss. "Does Alec beat up anyone who yells at you?"

"No one's ever yelled at me. At least not in front of Alec." Raine paused. "And, actually, no, people don't tend to yell at me."

"That's because you're sweet and kind," said Charlotte, only half joking.

"I'm starting to think it's because I have a pit bull for a brother."

Charlotte laughed. "You think he warned them off?"

"Maybe. But let's get back to the kiss. Tell me about it."

"Nothing to tell," Charlotte lied. It had been a kiss for the record books, and she'd been avoiding Alec ever since.

"Where were you? How did it happen?"

"We were on the balcony at one of the rental houses."

"And he just up and kissed you?"

"He thought I was crying."

Raine frowned. "That doesn't sound right."

"I was actually laughing," said Charlotte, forcing her mind to back away from the memory.

"Alec doesn't give sympathy kisses."

"You know about *all* his kisses, do you?"

"I have heard tales."

"Well, you're not going to hear any more tales from me." Charlotte sighed and got to her feet. "I'd better get out there and see what's going on. Alec's right. I did promise to take care of things." She picked up her purse. "I guess our fun's over."

"Uh-uh." Raine shook her head in denial. "I'm definitely going to talk to him."

"Oh, no, you don't," Charlotte protested. She had a job to do here, and she was going to take care of it.

"You don't need to watch every move they make," said Raine. "I'm not going to let him keep you prisoner here for weeks on end."

"*I'll* talk to him," said Charlotte. "Later." After Alec had a chance to calm down, they'd have a discussion and set out the parameters of her role in the film. She had an obligation to him, and she was going to live up to it.

Five

Filming went on until eight o'clock that night. Alec requested dinner in his office, not wanting to inflict his foul mood on anyone else. He'd signed up as a film location—a stupid decision, obviously. But it was a decision he'd made, and now he was going to have to live with it.

Things hadn't turned out exactly as he'd planned, but that was life. He'd leave for Tokyo in the morning. Might as well roll up his sleeves and ensure the new bicycle line launch came off without a hitch. He could also make a stop in New Delhi and touch base with the high-tech division.

There was always a long list of social events he should attend. Maybe he'd find a plain-Jane date, get his picture taken, make Kiefer happy. He might as well make somebody happy, because it sure wasn't going to be him, not if he stayed here.

There was a light tap on his office door.

"*Oui,* Henri?"

The door cracked open.

"It's Charlotte."

Oh, good. Now he could apologize on top of everything else. He sighed and came to his feet. *"Entrée."*

She slipped into the room, closed the door behind her and leaned against it. She was drop-dead gorgeous in a jazzy gold spaghetti-strap cocktail dress. Its vertical streaks shimmered against her toned thighs.

The wide, mahogany desk and two padded guest chairs formed a barrier between them. Just as well.

"They're going to replace the driveway," she finally said.

He moved around the desk, drawn to her. "It wasn't about the driveway."

She nodded her understanding. "Still. They broke it, they'll replace it."

"I take it you've been doing your job this afternoon?"

"I was."

"I appreciate that." What he really appreciated was that she was standing here in front of him, and they were alone for the first time in days.

"It was part of the deal."

"I was angry because you stayed away," he admitted, moving closer still, marveling that she grew more beautiful with each step.

"I've been here every day."

"With Raine glued to your side. Where is my sister, by the way?"

"She had to do something with Kiefer."

"At the office?"

Charlotte nodded.

Alec came to a halt in front of her. "And Jack?"

"At the hotel. With the crew."

Tokyo faded from his mind as Alec stroked his thumb over the fabric of her dress. He discovered the shimmer came from ribbons, beads and sequins. There was a weight and fullness to the dress that felt good under his hand. It had a double hem—scalloped over straight. It was a perfect dress for dancing.

Her long legs flowed down into strappy gold sandals. And the gold hoops dangling from her ears set off her shiny blond hair.

"You know," he told her softly, reframing his mood. "We all did something wrong."

She tipped her head questioningly.

"You shouldn't have stayed away. I shouldn't have yelled. And Jack should have decked me."

That got a smile from her. "Jack thinks you're crazy."

"He needs to learn how to be your brother."

"I can only hope that doesn't involve too many fist-fights."

Alec closed his hand around her rib cage, feeling the texture of the dress tickle his palm.

"I missed you," he admitted.

She closed her eyes for a long second. "Are we deep into the complicated end of the relationship spectrum?"

"It's simple from where I'm standing." He gazed at her creamy shoulders, the delicate straps of the dress, thinking how easy it would be to roll one off and press his lips against the warm fragrance of her skin.

"You're gorgeous," he elaborated. "I can't keep my hands off you. And there's *finally* nobody else here."

He slipped his index finger under the strap, sliding it back and forth. "What could be simpler than that?"

"I came here to talk to you about expectations."

He smiled. "I hope you won't be disappointed."

"I mean my job here. For the film. I don't want to let you down again."

"Forget it."

She searched his expression. "I don't know what that means."

"It means I wasn't angry about the driveway. I wasn't angry you had fun with Raine. I was angry because you weren't in my bed. And that's not a fair reason to be angry."

She stilled. Not breathing, staring up at him with desire, trepidation and anticipation all mixed up together.

His hand tightened, drawing her in. He bent his head, parted his lips and met hers in a slow, gentle exploration.

Last time had been too hurried. He'd behaved like a teenager, not giving a thought to savoring the moment, to making sure she felt cherished, to kissing her the way a Frenchman should kiss, the way a Frenchman ought to approach everything in life.

She tasted of fine wine, his own vintage. Her lips were soft and smooth, warm and malleable under his. She was kissing him back, and passion uncoiled within him. His forearm went to the small of her back, pressing her soft curves against his firm body. She was ambrosia, a gift from the gods, an angel set down on earth for him and him alone.

Her tongue flicked against his lips, kicking a jolt of desire from his body to his brain. He struggled to keep it slow, but his mouth was moving of its own accord, delving deeper, kissing harder, bending her backward so that her body arched into his own.

Blood rushed through his system, priming his body, challenging reason. Her hands gripped his shoulders, while small moans worked their way from her chest to her mouth. His lips moved to her neck, and she arched back farther. Her breasts were taut against the dress, cleavage bursting from the V-neck, her nipples outlined against the fabric.

His hand covered one breast, and they both gasped in wonder. He drew his thumb over the peak, and her knees buckled. He held her steady, whispering words of endearment and encouragement.

He lifted her, wrapping her legs around his waist, pushing her dress out of the way and pressing her against the solid door. He took her mouth once more, kissing her deeply. His hands roamed from her breasts to her waist to her bare thighs revealed by the bunched dress. When he touched the lace of her panties, she hissed out a yes.

Her hands cupped his face, and she covered him with tiny kisses. She drew his earlobe into her hot mouth, and his body nearly jackknifed in shock. He slipped his thumb between her legs, over the silk of her panties. She was hot and moist and delectably sweet.

There were condoms in the bathroom adjoining the office. He cradled her bottom, lifting her away from the door, carrying her to the en suite, all the while kissing, caressing and assuring her she was the most beautiful woman in the world.

Inside, he perched her on the counter, stripped off his slacks and the scrap of her panties, donned the

condom, then stepped between her legs. The counter
was the right height, and their bodies touched intimately.

He smoothed back her hair and gazed into her eyes.
Then he drew his thumb along her swollen bottom lip,
following it up with his mouth, drawing her lip inside,
tasting her essence as his hands roamed lower.

She squirmed forward, bringing his fingers in
contact with the fire between her legs. Her hands fisted
in his hair, and her moaning little pants heated his ear.

He parted her flesh.

"Now?" he asked.

"Right now," she gasped in return, and he pushed
inside.

She arched back, and he anchored his hands at the
base of her spine, pressing her forward, refining his
angle, savoring the feel of her body for long moments
before he withdrew. Then he pushed in again, swifter,
harder.

Her eyes were closed, and sweat dotted her hairline. Her skin was slick and fragrant against his. Her
dress rustled against the counter. He drew down the
neckline, revealing her breasts, closing his mouth
over one pert nipple, laving it, drawing hard, elicit-
ing a groan as her hands tightened and her fingernails
dug into his upper arms.

He moved to the other breast, repeating the motion.

Her eyes were scrunched tight. Her hips arched,
her body matching his motion. He wished he could
rip off the dress and see her naked. But there was no
time for that.

His speed increased of its own accord, and her
keening cries made his brain buzz with need. There

was nothing left but a roar of desire and a primal need to take them both to the clouds and over the edge and straight into eternal paradise.

He wrapped his arms around her, holding her close as the tremors shook both of their bodies and heat drenched their skin.

Charlotte lay in the tangled sheets of Alec's big bed. Her cheek rested on his chest, and his breathing was even and strong. A breeze flowed through the open, third-floor window, billowing sheer curtains and revealing the garden lights below.

"I guess we should probably keep this a secret," she ventured.

"You think?" He trailed his fingertips lightly down her bare arm. "Or should we let Kiefer in with the camera?"

"Or we could hold a press conference right here in the bed like John and Yoko?"

"I can guarantee you the front page."

She turned her head, resting her chin on his shoulder. "Seriously."

He gazed into her eyes. "Seriously. It's our secret."

She nodded.

"What about Jack?"

Charlotte frowned, not understanding.

"Are you going to tell Jack?"

"No." Her brother had never been privy to her love life before. "Are you going to tell Raine?"

Alec shrugged. "Your call."

"She's suspicious, you know."

"Really?"

"After you yelled at me this afternoon, she asked if

you'd made a pass at me. She thought you were mad because I'd turned you down."

"She's not far off the mark," he said.

"I told her we'd kissed." Charlotte settled more comfortably against Alec's chest, toying with the edge of the white sheet.

"Are you going to tell her…" His voice trailed off.

Charlotte didn't exactly know what to call it, either. A one-night stand? A fling?

But one thing she did know, she wasn't going to get all needy on him and start demanding to know what this meant and where it was going. She'd gone into it with her eyes wide open. She knew what and who Alec was, but she'd hopped into his bed anyway.

"It's better if she doesn't know," Charlotte admitted. "But I don't want to lie to her. My grandfather—" She stopped.

She wasn't going to start borrowing trouble here. Her grandfather didn't need to find out. Nobody needed to find out. Unless Alec was a complete cad, and she certainly didn't think he was, this interlude would remain locked in her heart forever.

"How long have you worked for the ambassador?" Alec asked, obviously prepared to move on.

She followed his lead. "Since I was a teenager. I started off helping in the office. Then, after college, I worked full-time. And when his executive assistant quit to get married, I stepped in temporarily."

"When was that?"

"Three years ago. Right before I met you the first time."

"Ahh." He nodded. "Rome. You should have taken my key that night."

"Right. And I'd have made the front page, scandalized my family and been fired from my job."

Alec paused. "That's altogether a worst-case scenario, isn't it?"

"It's a likely-case scenario. You nearly ruined my life."

"Good that we waited, then." He placed a gentle kiss on her forehead, gathering her close. "Honestly—right now, I'm very, very glad we waited."

Charlotte didn't know what to say to that. He made it sound as if they'd done it deliberately, as if they'd had some kind of connection, as if they'd been thinking about each other over the past three years. Had he thought about her after Rome? Did he even remember her in the long line of women he flirted with?

She gave herself a mental shake. She wasn't going to make more of this than there was.

"Is Kiefer still worried about rumors of you and Isabella?" she asked, moving on.

"We seem to have an ally in Ridley Sinclair."

"We do?" Charlotte hadn't even met the man yet.

"I hear he generally has an affair with his costar."

Interesting. "And he's staying in the same villa as Isabella?"

Alec nodded. "That he is."

"You think they'll have an affair?"

"Rumor has it they already are," said Alec. "Though that rumor may have been started by Kiefer."

Charlotte laughed. "I think I'm starting to like Kiefer."

"You be careful of Kiefer." There was a serious note in Alec's tone that caused Charlotte to twist to look him in the eyes again.

"What do you mean?"

"I mean Kiefer has a way with women."

"And you don't?" She glanced down at her naked body, the twisted sheets, the comforter that had been kicked off the bed an hour ago. If she needed to be careful of anybody here, it was Alec.

"I hear your father's due tomorrow." Alec changed the subject. She didn't blame him. What more was there to say?

"I heard that Lars has a few more days of second-unit work," said Charlotte. "But they want to start rehearsals for the major scenes."

"Will it bother you?"

"The major scenes?" Charlotte expected it to become even more chaotic at the château. But they'd known this was coming.

"Seeing your father. Is it worse than seeing Jack?"

"It's nowhere near the same," said Charlotte, burrowing farther beneath the sheet to combat a growing chill from the open window.

Alec reached to the floor and retrieved the comforter, spreading it over both of them.

"Thanks." She sighed as their body heat formed a warm cocoon.

"Your father?" Alec prompted.

"It's funny," she admitted. "I think I always knew David was a terrible father. Even when my mom was alive, he was never around. When she died, I honestly thought it would be Jack who took care of me."

"How old was Jack?"

"Nine. But he seemed very worldly wise. He used to pour me juice, make me sandwiches and read me bedtime stories." She smiled wistfully at the memory.

"And then he abandoned you."

"No, he didn't." She knew none of it had been Jack's fault. "But for years, I expected him to come and get me. I don't know what I thought, that he'd turn eleven, get a paper route and we'd live happily ever after. Pretty absurd, huh?"

Alec straightened the comforter around her. "You were a little girl."

"Who took a very long time to wake up to reality."

"Do you think you might be angry with him?"

She shook her head. "I missed him. That was all." She still missed him. She wanted a brother, and what she had was an acquaintance.

"Tell me about you and Raine." Charlotte knew she should go back to her own room before anyone else got home, but she didn't want to leave. She didn't want it to end just yet. "Did you protect her? Tease her? Gang up with her against your parents?"

Alec chuckled. "I was Raine's worst night—"

A deafening boom shook the château. Orange flames lit up the sky. Alec instantly threw himself on top of Charlotte, bracing her protectively against the bed.

"What the hell?" he ground out, glancing to the window behind him.

Charlotte blinked at the fire, smoke and ash rising toward the dark sky.

"You okay?" he demanded.

Her ears were ringing, and she'd experienced an adrenaline shot strong enough to stun an ox, but she nodded jerkily.

Alec sprang from the bed, crossing to the window while he stuffed his legs into his slacks. "Good God. One of the trailers is on fire."

"It blew up?" Charlotte stated the obvious as she

clambered out of bed herself, glancing around for her dress and shoes.

He dialed his cell phone with one hand, pulling his dress shirt on with the other as he headed for the bedroom door. There, he paused. "Will you be all right?"

"I'll be fine," she called. She could hear sirens in the distance, and people were shouting down on the lawn.

She prayed that nobody had been hurt. But the sirens were getting closer, and the shouts were getting louder. She struggled into her dress and into her shoes, then she clattered down the stairs to find out if she could help.

The front lawn looked like a disaster zone. Staff members and crew rushed to the aid of those lying on the ground. Alec was in the middle, shouting to his staff to bring blankets and first aid, while helping the gardeners to set up hoses to soak the semitrailers and a small cottage that were next to the fire.

Charlotte stopped, unsure of what to do.

She glanced at the man next to her. His face was black with soot, and he was cradling his left arm, his sleeve covered in blood.

"You're hurt," she stated, moving closer.

He looked down at his arm. "It's just a cut."

"Anything else?" She gingerly supported him on the uninjured side, helping him to the porch where he could sit down.

"It was the FX trailer," he rasped.

She separated the torn sleeve, revealing a long, deep cut on his forearm.

"They were getting the pyrotechnics ready for the battle scene." The man seemed to be in shock.

Charlotte's gaze shifted involuntarily to the burning

trailer. Alec was silhouetted against the flames. The fire trucks arrived, and he signaled them forward, clearing people out of their path as the firefighters jumped down and began connecting hoses.

If anybody had been inside…

A member of the housekeeping staff appeared, and Charlotte quickly latched on to a couple of towels and a bottle of water. She soaked one towel, carefully cleaning around the wound. Then she pressed the other towel against the cut, applying pressure to stop the bleeding.

"Am I hurting you?" she asked.

The man barely shook his head, his attention fixed on the firefighters and the approaching ambulances.

The attendants ran to a couple of people lying on the ground, and Charlotte wasn't sure whether she should flag them down.

"I can wait," the man said, guessing her thoughts.

"Are you sure?" The towel was soaking up a lot of blood.

"Charlotte?" It was Raine's voice.

Charlotte looked into Raine's stark expression.

"What *happened?* We just got back—"

"Can you get us a paramedic?"

Raine's gaze jumped to the injured man. "Of course."

She scooted across the lawn in her skirt and high heels. She stopped a woman in uniform and pointed to Charlotte. The woman grabbed a black case and trotted toward them.

"Thank you," said Charlotte as the woman knelt down.

"I'm fine," said the man.

"Let's take a quick look," said the attendant, swiftly removing the towel.

She opened the case and retrieved gauze, disinfectant and medical tape.

"I'll be sending you in for some stitches," she told the man.

He simply nodded, looking exhausted.

"What happened?" Raine repeated.

"The FX trailer blew up," Charlotte told her.

Raine's voice went hushed. "Anybody inside?"

Charlotte looked to the ambulance attendant.

The woman shrugged.

"We made it out," said the man, and all three women looked at him.

"We…" His eyelids fluttered rapidly, and the blood drained from his face.

"Mon dieu." The attendant quickly laid him prone, raising his feet. "Shock," she told them, then lifted her radio mic. "Etienne? Can you bring a stretcher?"

Her radio crackled something unintelligible in response.

"Have you seen Alec?" asked Raine as the stretcher clattered toward them.

"He was hosing down buildings." Charlotte peered into the gloom. The trailer was beaten down to a glowing pile of rubble. The other trailers and the shed were still standing. The lawn was a mud bog, and the surrounding flower beds were completely in ruins.

Charlotte's stomach turned hollow. She was causing the destruction of Alec's home. "I can't believe this," she whispered.

"Freak accident," said Raine, gazing around.

The man with the stretcher came to a halt.

"Fatalities?" asked the female attendant, attracting Charlotte and Raine's attention.

The man shook his head. "It sounds like there were three people in the trailer. They all got out. One broken arm. One concussion. Some superficial burns. And this one." He nodded to the man who was still unconscious on the porch.

"He'll need some stitches. We should start an IV and get a blood-pressure reading."

The two counted off, hoisting the man onto the stretcher, securing straps and hooking up tubes.

"He's going to be fine," the female attendant told Charlotte.

"Thank you." Too bad the same couldn't be said for Alec's front yard.

"It's not your fault," said Raine as they wheeled the man away.

"I *promised* him nothing would go wrong."

"Did you set off the explosion?"

"No."

"Then Alec will understand."

Charlotte watched Alec talking to the fire chief. His hands were waving, his face contorted and he was talking fast and emphatically. He didn't look as if he understood much of anything.

"We can replant the flowers," said Raine. "Haul away the rubble."

"Fire me," said Charlotte with a sigh of defeat. She really didn't want to face Alec's anger, particularly after she'd seen such a very different side of him.

"You're a volunteer," Raine pointed out. "I don't think we can fire you."

"Do you think he'll back out of the deal?" Butterflies formed in Charlotte's stomach as Alec started toward them, eyes hard, mouth pulled in a grim line.

"I think we're about to find out," said Raine.

Charlotte moved slightly closer to Raine for protection as Alec marched ominously toward them. Her heart rate seemed to increase with every step he took. His hands were dirty, his clothing soaked to his skin, and his face was streaked with soot and sweat.

He looked ruggedly sexy. Except for the scowl. Okay, even with the scowl, he looked sexy. She was hopeless.

He came to a halt. "No one was seriously hurt."

"I'm so sorry," said Charlotte.

Alec's eyes narrowed, and she assumed it was going to take a whole lot more than an apology.

"Do they know what happened?" asked Raine.

"Some kind of electrical malfunction with the pyrotechnics. It's going to put them behind schedule." He glanced around in disgust, and Charlotte figured the movie schedule was hardly his first concern.

He looked to Charlotte. "Can I talk to you alone?"

"It's not her fault," Raine jumped in.

Alec gave his sister a look that questioned her sanity.

Charlotte supposed it was her fault. And she didn't blame Alec for being angry. She was ready to face the music. But she was sorely disappointed at having let the Hudsons down.

Alec reached for her arm, then he seemed to remember his filthy hands, because he pulled back, nodding toward a quiet corner of the porch.

"I feel terrible," she began as soon as they were out of earshot. "I should have thought about security. I should have thought about safety—"

"I need to ask," said Alec, coming to a halt, turning to face her. He didn't look angry. In fact, he looked concerned.

"What?" she asked bravely, watching his expression closely.

"What happened earlier—between us."

Ahh. Now she got it. She shifted gears. This was the it-was-a-good-time speech, the we're-both-adults speech, the no-expectations speech.

Okay. She was prepared for that. They *were* both adults, and neither of them were under any illusions.

Charlotte squared her shoulders. "You don't have to say it, Alec. I understand. And I agree with you completely." They'd go on as if nothing had happened. If he'd let them stay and complete the movie, that was a huge win for her. She wasn't going to sit around and cry over a one-night stand.

Well, maybe she'd cry a bit. But only because it was such an incredible one-night stand. It would have been nice for it to be two nights or three. But that wasn't the way Alec operated. Or so she'd read in the tabloids.

"You agree with me?" he asked.

She nodded. "And it'll stay our secret."

He folded his arms over his wet shirt. "We already established that."

"Right." She nodded. "Of course we did." So what was left to talk about?

"What I wanted to ask you…" He glanced around. Then he moved in closer. "Do you want to do it again?"

Charlotte blinked. "I don't understand."

He moved closer still. "I don't dare even touch you out here, never mind pull you into my arms and kiss you. But I'm asking, do you want to make love with me again?"

"*And* finish the movie?"

"What does one have to do with the other?"

"Well, I'm here because of the filming, and now we've destroyed your yard."

He glanced over her shoulder. "They did a pretty good job of that."

"Are you kicking us out?"

"No."

"Why not?"

He sighed. "Do you have any idea how hard it is for me to stand here and keep my hands off you?"

Charlotte had a pretty good idea, since she was fighting the same battle to keep her hands off him. She smiled.

He frowned in return. "Answer the damn question."

"Yes."

"Good."

"Raine is staring at us."

"You let me worry about Raine."

Six

Charlotte changed out of her dress and took a long, hot shower. Afterward, she was still too keyed up to sleep. It was past midnight, but people were still working in the yard. Equipment roared to life, and a few firefighters stood by the smoking rubble with shovels and a hose.

She slipped into a pair of jeans and a short T-shirt, stuffing her feet into a pair of low sandals and pulling her damp hair into a simple ponytail.

Maybe she could find some brandy in the kitchen. A strong drink might help her sleep.

She padded down two flights of stairs, past the film sets in the entryway and the great room, along the hall toward the back of the house. She heard voices through the open door of a library.

Alec, Kiefer, Jack, Lars and three other crew members sat around a large table.

"David will be here in the morning to do an assessment," said Jack, slipping his cell phone into his pocket.

"We'll lose two shooting days at least," said Lars with a scowl. "Somebody's ass is on the—"

"I can pull a construction crew off the project in Toulouse," Kiefer said to Alec.

Charlotte cringed. Alec had been clear that none of his employees were to be impacted.

"I don't think it's necessary to fire anyone," said Alec, staring directly at Lars. "Seems to me you're going to need all the skilled labor you can find."

The three crew members stilled, and Lars's mouth worked as his face went ruddy. "How is it any of your—"

"It's my yard that was burned to a crisp," said Alec. "And I don't intend it to become a permanent movie set."

"We move on," said Jack, nodding in Alec's direction, clearly overruling Lars. "Accidents happen."

It was the first time Charlotte had seen her brother pull rank. Maybe it was because she didn't particularly like Lars. Or maybe it was because he was backing Alec. But she was proud of Jack.

Alec caught sight of her. He gave her a little smile and motioned her in, indicating an empty chair next to him.

"The construction crew?" Kiefer asked Alec.

"If we can spare them," said Alec, letting his thigh come to rest against Charlotte's as she sat down. He had also changed, into a pair of black slacks and a royal-blue, pin-striped dress shirt. He hadn't bothered with a tie, and she discovered she liked the casual look on him.

"Send me the bill," Jack told Kiefer.

Kiefer gave him a nod.

Lars was silent and sullen, his jaw clenched where he'd pulled back from the table.

One of the other crew members flipped through a clipboard. "If we switch scenes thirty-five and sixteen, and move up the party sequence, we can make up some time," he said.

"Can you get the extras in tomorrow?" asked Jack.

"On it," said the man, making a notation.

"The story editor isn't finished with thirty-five," said Lars.

"He has eight hours to *get* finished," said Jack.

"Unacceptable," Lars retorted.

"You want to duke it out with David tomorrow?" asked Jack, a tightness around his mouth. "Because I'm not about to tell a man coming off a string of low-budget independents that our story editor is a prima donna."

Alec leaned over to Charlotte and whispered, "I think Jack has this well in hand."

She tried not to smile. She'd always assumed Jack's laid-back persona meant he wasn't as strong as some of those around him. He might disguise it, but her brother seemed to have a backbone of steel.

"Charlotte?" came Raine's voice from the doorway.

Charlotte guiltily snapped her leg away from Alec's and pushed back her chair.

"I was looking for you," she said to Raine, coming to her feet. She crossed the room without looking back. "I was hoping to find some brandy," she told Raine in an undertone.

"Right this way," said Raine, pointing to the kitchen. She was still wearing the kicky little black skirt with a fitted, purple tank top. Charlotte couldn't help wondering what Raine had been doing for the past hour.

She settled into a breakfast nook, while Raine rattled through a cabinet.

The bay window faced east, so the destruction of the front yard was out of sight. The moon was full, the stars in multiple layers. Pot lights outlined a few of the garden pathways, and the pool was just visible down the slope, beyond an oleander hedge.

"I know I won't sleep, either," said Raine, curling onto the semicircular bench seat across from Charlotte. She set down a bottle of cognac and two thin crystal snifters.

"I'm so glad nobody was seriously hurt," said Charlotte.

"Now that out there," said Raine, pouring the amber liquid into the glasses, "that was more like the real Alec."

"He took it very well," Charlotte agreed. Though she supposed two hours of vigorous sex might have mellowed him out a little. "What were you doing with Kiefer?"

"We're renovating the head office in Toulouse. The architect wanted to change the configuration of my offices."

"Problem?"

Raine grinned. "Not really. But don't tell Kiefer."

"You're making him sweat?"

Raine nodded.

"Just recreationally?" Charlotte took a sip of the cognac, letting the warm liquid ease down her throat.

"You bet," said Raine with a toss of her bobbed hair. "Life's too easy for Kiefer."

"And it's not for you?"

Raine frowned. "It's not the same thing. I don't have every woman in France laying out the red carpet for me."

"You're his boss."

"Ha! I'd love to hear you say that when Kiefer's in the room."

"Say what when Kiefer's in the room?" Kiefer appeared from the hallway.

Charlotte glanced to Raine, unsure of what to say.

"Go ahead." Raine laughed. "Tell him."

Charlotte cleared her throat, trying to guess what kind of a hornet's nest she was walking into. "That she's your boss."

Kiefer scoffed out a strangled laugh. "Not until she can read a balance sheet, write a contract or take me in a fistfight."

"I own fifty percent of Montcalm Corporation."

"We both know that's an honorary thing." His gaze zeroed in on the bottle, and he helped himself to a snifter from a glassed-in cupboard.

"See what I have to put up with?" Raine asked Charlotte.

"Do you have signing authority?" asked Charlotte, taking Raine's side. She liked Kiefer, but she assumed he could take care of himself.

"I have plenty of signing authority." Raine nodded briskly.

"Alec is the CEO," Kiefer pointed out. "And I have absolutely no problem reporting to him."

"I don't know, Kiefer," Charlotte teased. "If she can sign your paycheck, I think you work for her."

Kiefer poured himself a measure of cognac. "When she has the power to fire me, I'll get worried."

"You're fired," said Raine.

Kiefer just chuckled, holding up his brandy in a toast. "You just keep publishing the pretty little puff pictures, sweetheart. Let me worry about the serious stuff."

Raine's jade eyes flared, and she jumped to her feet. "I can't get any respect. I swear, I am getting an MBA."

But Charlotte's attention stayed on Kiefer, watching his expression, catching that unguarded second when his gaze dipped to Raine's clingy, low-cut top and his nostrils flared.

Charlotte sat back. *Interesting.* The crackling energy between them was a lot more than just antagonism.

"Good luck with that," Kiefer drawled.

"If only to shove it in your face."

"Your degree is in what?" he asked mildly. "Fashion? Fine art?"

"*That's* why I'm a magazine publisher."

He swirled the cognac in his wide palm, pretending to study it. "By the way—" he looked up "—circulation was down last quarter."

"You're an ass."

"Hey—" he feigned innocence "—don't shoot the messenger."

"Don't ask me to do this, Alec." On the balcony of Alec's office, Kiefer gazed down at the construction crew swarming over last night's fire rubble.

"It's a couple of days," said Alec from the open doorway, struggling to understand why Kiefer would refuse. "Take her to the distribution offices. Meet with the executives."

"Raine doesn't need me there."

"I want you to get a feel for the magazine business. You said yourself distribution was down."

"Marginally."

Alec stepped out onto the balcony, moving next to Kiefer at the rail.

"You need me here," said Kiefer.

"No, we don't."

"Or in Toulouse."

"What good are you in Toulouse? The office is a mess, and the construction crew is working here."

"Tokyo, then. Send me to Kana Hanako."

"I want you to help Raine." Truth was, Alec wanted Kiefer to make sure Raine stayed away from the château for a couple of days. It was the only way he was going to get any time alone with Charlotte.

Underhanded, maybe. But he had used Kiefer for less noble purposes in the past.

Kiefer's jaw set in a line, and his hands smacked down hard on the rail. "Well, you might as well fire me, then." He turned to stalk back into the office.

What?

Alec gave his head a shake.

"What?" He shifted to stare at Kiefer.

Kiefer rounded, his hands on his hips. "Go ahead. Fire me for refusing an order."

"I'm not—" Alec stepped inside. "Listen, I know you're not wild about Raine."

Kiefer started to laugh.

"What's funny?"

"I'm not *wild* about Raine?"

Okay, so Raine made Kiefer nuts. They'd always sparked off each other, dragged one another down into the most petty of arguments. But they'd worked together for years. Alec assumed the relationship was at least tolerable.

Kiefer took a step forward, shaking his head in

amazement. "You think I'm refusing an order because I don't like Raine?"

"Why else?" It was not as if traveling to Paris, London and Rome was some kind of hardship. Particularly if they took the corporate jet.

Kiefer stared hard at Alec, a debate obviously going on inside his head.

"Kiefer?" Alec prompted.

"I *am* wild about Raine."

Alec didn't understand.

Kiefer gave another cold laugh. His fists clenched by his sides. "I'd rather you fired me for refusing an order than fire me for sleeping with your sister."

"Huh?" Alec was honestly speechless.

"Your sister's hot, Alec. She gorgeous. She's sexy—"

"But you two fight all the time."

"That's because if we stop fighting—" Kiefer clamped his jaw.

Alec struggled to reframe his thoughts. Kiefer and Raine? Raine and Kiefer? "You've known her for years. Surely you can keep your hands off her for a few more days."

"We've never traveled alone together."

"That's just crazy," said Alec, refusing to believe Kiefer would completely disregard his professional ethics.

"She's had a crush on me since she was eighteen," said Kiefer. "I'm not stupid. She hides it, because she hates herself for it—"

"Then she'll say no," Alec pointed out. "And I know you'll respect that. If you make a move, Raine will simply turn you down."

"Don't count on her saying no."

Alec struggled with a sudden burst of temper. His vice president was actually standing there telling him he planned to seduce his sister?

"Just fire me now," said Kiefer, throwing up his hands in disgust.

"Nobody's getting fired."

"Then forget about the trip."

"I can't forget about the trip."

"Why the hell not? Circulation took a minuscule dip. If you insist, we'll follow it up. But we can call the offices. It's not even worth the jet fuel—" Kiefer stopped. His chin suddenly dipped to his chest. He stared at Alec out of the tops of his eyes. Then he shook his head in disgust. "You need Raine out of the house."

Alec couldn't lie, so he stayed silent.

"It's Charlotte, isn't it? You want me to babysit Raine so that you can seduce Charlotte." Kiefer rapped his knuckles on the desktop. "Charlotte has a brother, too, you know."

"Jack has nothing to do with this. Charlotte's a grown woman."

"Yeah," said Kiefer. "So is Raine."

Alec was forced to agree. And that was a sobering thought for both men. It meant Raine's love life was none of his business. It meant Kiefer had held back all these years for no reason. It meant if Kiefer took Raine off in the jet, whatever happened between them was entirely their business.

"Yes," Alec finally answered. "She is."

The two men stared at each other in silence.

"And you still want me to take her around Europe?"

"If what you say is true, it's about time you two settled it one way or the other."

Kiefer gave a nod.

"I can count on your ethics?" Alec confirmed.

"*Everything* will be her call."

"Something to give me confidence," said Charlotte, staring into the depths of Raine's massive clothes closet.

"How about a jacket?" asked Raine, reaching for a couple of hangers. "Cropped? Classic?" She held up two.

"You have anything in white?" asked Charlotte. "I think white makes a statement."

"I'm not afraid of getting dirty? Even in the aftermath of a fire?"

"Exactly." Charlotte moved to get a better view of the skirts hanging in Raine's closet. The two women were close enough to the same size that she could borrow clothes. "I'd like to look crisp and professional."

Raine lowered her voice. "Are you nervous?"

Charlotte shrugged. "Isabella and Ridley are due on set today. David will show up, for sure—"

"Your father, David?"

"Right. My father, David. And Devlin and Max— two cousins—won't be far behind."

Raine turned and cocked her head. "You know, Charlotte, you are an incredibly successful, intelligent, beautiful woman."

"Thank you."

"I mean it. You've got nothing to prove. You shouldn't let them do this to you."

Charlotte turned her attention to a white, pleated skirt, trying to formulate her thoughts.

"*They* should be worried about impressing *you*," said Raine with staunch loyalty.

Charlotte laughed. "They're the Hudsons of Hollywood. They impress people simply by breathing."

There was a knock on the bedroom door.

"Come in," Raine called.

The door opened and Charlotte saw Kiefer. "You decent in there?" he called to Raine in the depth of the closet, studiously focusing on a bay window.

"No. I'm naked," stated Raine. "That's why I called you in." She brushed past Charlotte, her demeanor instantly prickly.

Charlotte hid a smile at Raine's habit of going overboard to hide her attraction to Kiefer.

Kiefer frowned at her sarcasm. "I was merely trying to be a gentleman."

"Why start now?" Raine responded tartly.

Charlotte made her way out of the closet.

"Your brother wants us to go to Rome."

Raine's brows went up. "Us?"

"You and me. And to Paris and London. He's worried about the circulation numbers."

"Tell him I'll get more data. Charlotte's here. I'm not going to Rome."

"He insists," said Kiefer. "Believe me when I tell you, I'm less thrilled than you."

"I doubt that," said Raine.

"He wants us to talk to the *Intérêt* distributors and come up with a game plan."

"Why now?"

"Because *now* is when the numbers are slipping."

Raine heaved a sigh.

"Buck up," said Kiefer, glancing at the three jackets draped over Raine's arm. "Maybe you can fit in a little clothes shopping."

Raine suddenly smiled. "What a great idea." She turned to Charlotte. "You can come with us to Rome. Via Condotti, Via Frattina. We'll have a blast."

"I don't—" Kiefer began. But Raine held up a hand to forestall him.

"It's decided," she pronounced. "If you're going to drag me to Rome, Charlotte and I will make a shopping trip of it."

Charlotte had to admit, the idea had merit. While she could borrow Raine's clothes, they wore different shoe sizes. When she packed for this trip, she'd expected to be staying two or three days. She definitely needed to upgrade her wardrobe.

Besides, getting out of Provence for a few days would mean she could put off meeting up with the Hudson clan. Although she told herself she could handle it, her stomach had been churning all morning. A few new outfits from Italy couldn't hurt her confidence.

Alec appeared in the doorway, his gaze darting from Raine to Kiefer, then settling on Charlotte. His expression stayed neutral, but gold flecks flared in his brown eyes, sending a shiver of remembrance zipping along her spine.

"Great news," said Raine, and Alec's expression turned puzzled.

"Charlotte's coming on the trip with us. We're going *shopping*."

Alec's horrified gaze shot to Kiefer.

"Raine's idea," said Kiefer defensively.

"Charlotte can't go with you," Alec quickly put in. "She has to stay with the film."

Raine waved a dismissive hand. "She's not in jail. Besides, what's left to blow up?"

"I really wish you hadn't said that," Kiefer deadpanned.

"I need Charlotte here," Alec insisted, and it instantly dawned on Charlotte that Alec was staying here.

Another look passed between Alec and Kiefer, and Charlotte realized it was a setup. Kiefer had been assigned to get Raine out of the way, so Alec could spend time with her.

Charlotte wouldn't lie to herself, she was keen to spend time with Alec, too. But talk about an over-the-top move by a self-indulgent man—sending his own sister on a wild-goose chase.

"I'd really rather go to Rome," she put in, giving Alec a defiant stare.

"See?" Raine jumped in. "The poor woman needs a wardrobe."

"Yeah," Charlotte agreed, "this poor woman needs a wardrobe."

Alec glared at her, clearly trying to transmit a message. She understood just fine. She simply wasn't going to be a party to his machinations.

"Fine," Alec ground out. "I'll come, too."

That surprised Charlotte. And judging by their expressions, it surprised Raine and Kiefer, as well.

"That's ridicu—" Something in Alec's eyes stopped Kiefer cold. "Great idea," Kiefer said instead. "The four of us, shopping together in Rome. What could be more fun?"

Charlotte wasn't sure about fun. But it was definitely going to be interesting.

Charlotte showed Alec no mercy. While Raine and Kiefer visited the magazine distributor in Rome, she dragged him to the shopping district. They visited Versace, Dolce & Gabbana, Ferragamo and Biagiotti, along with a dozen other shops and boutiques on the famous Italian streets.

Enjoying herself, she found beachwear, jeans, a couple of funky little jackets, three great party dresses and a formal gown for an upcoming event with her grandfather. She also picked out a new purse and a few pieces of jewelry. She'd fought Alec for the right to pay at every store. He was quick on the credit card draw, but she managed to either outsmart or outmaneuver him every time.

"Intimate apparel?" he asked, glancing skeptically at the discreet sign above the glass door on the stone face of the building.

He'd been patient so far, but she considered this the ultimate test. "A girl does need underwear."

"You think this is funny?"

In fact, she did. "You intimidated?"

"By women's underwear? Bring it on." He pulled open the door and stood back to let her enter.

Alec found a seat in a small lounge area and picked up a magazine. A sales associate quickly appeared and offered him coffee, which he accepted, hoisting the cup in a toast to Charlotte.

She held an elegant, full-length, white satin gown up against her body.

He frowned and shook his head.

She pointed to a frivolous pink bra and panties, decorated with white fur.

He rolled his eyes.

Scanning the small racks in front of her, she chose a short nightgown of subtly patterned purple silk, with a lace-inset front and spaghetti straps.

Alec gave her a thumbs-up. Then he waggled his eyebrows and pointed to a low-cut, lacy black camisole with a matching thong. It was obviously his turn to try to embarrass her.

She sauntered defiantly over and whisked the hanger from the rack.

He laughed silently and looked down at his magazine.

Charlotte moved farther back in the small store, selecting some more practical, though equally beautiful lingerie for everyday wear, then headed for a fitting room.

When she brought her selections to the saleswoman, Alec was there with his credit card.

"Not a chance," she muttered to him.

"My turn," he insisted.

"You're not buying my clothes," she told him, as the clerk glanced from one credit card to the next.

"I'm going to enjoy them every bit as much as you."

"Not if you keep this up," said Charlotte, and the clerk was forced to fight a grin.

Alec hesitated, and Charlotte moved quickly, pressing her credit card into the clerk's palm.

"I win," she sang.

He gazed down at the black camisole and thong on the counter. "Not necessarily."

As they had with her other purchases, they arranged to have them delivered to the hotel.

"Are we done?" asked Alec on the way out the door.

Charlotte pretended to consider. "That should keep me for a few days," she allowed.

"We still have London and Paris," he reminded her.

"Then I'm done for now," she said decisively.

"Thank goodness." He gently steered her south on the busy street.

"If you don't like shopping, why did you come?"

"Because *you*..." He smacked her smartly on the bottom.

"Hey!"

Two passing Italian men whistled their appreciation.

"...wouldn't stay home with me," Alec finished.

She blinked innocently up at him. "I was supposed to stay home?"

"Do you have any idea how much trouble it was to get Kiefer to take Raine out of our hair?"

"I can't believe it was hard at all. He's got the hots for her."

"You knew that?"

Charlotte scoffed out a laugh. "It's pretty obvious. Well, to everybody but Raine. She likes him, too, you know."

"So I hear."

"You playing matchmaker?" she asked.

"I wanted to see you alone. Those two can take care of themselves."

"And, here we are," noted Charlotte.

"You made me work hard enough."

"Serves you right. Pimping out your sister like that."

"Clearly, I'm shameless when it comes to you."

"Let's hope I'm worth it."

His voice lowered to an intimate tone. "Oh, I already know you're worth it."

While Charlotte told herself not to read too much into his words, they walked in silence along the narrow, cobblestone street amongst other couples and families out enjoying the sunshine and shopping. They came around a corner to the Tiber River.

Alec pointed to a marina of large, expensive-looking yachts. "We should rent a boat."

"You're joking." Talk about an extravagance.

"You have to see the river, particularly at sunset. The bridges, the statues. St. Peter's Basilica and the Castillo de San Angelo are absolutely magnificent."

"Look." It was her turn to point. "There's a patio café. We can see the river for the price of a cup of coffee."

Alec turned to stare at her in confusion. "You don't want to cruise?"

"I don't want to rent a yacht!"

"It's only money."

She took his hand. "Let's get a cup of coffee, then we'll walk a ways."

"Coffee?" he confirmed with obvious disappointment.

She nodded and pointed them toward the little café.

They found mesh, metal seats and a little metal table by the rail. The breeze was cool off the water, and a barge floated by, while compact cars made their way over an ancient stone bridge.

Before sitting down, Alec removed his jacket, putting it around Charlotte's shoulders. She smiled her thanks.

While he spoke to the waiter in Italian, Alec pulled out his own seat.

He sat down, his gaze soft on her face as he seemed to consider her. "You're different," he finally told her.

"Different from what?" The coat was still warm from his body heat, and it felt comforting around her body.

"From other women."

She toyed with the silverware on the table. "Is that a good thing or a bad thing?"

He sat back in his chair. "Ever since they estimated my net worth in *Forbes,* it's as if I have a bull's-eye painted in the middle of my back. A great big target for every woman who thinks her life would be improved by money."

"Were they right?"

His forehead creased. "The women?"

A tourist barge sounded its horn, and a group of partyers waved and shouted.

Charlotte waved in return. "*Forbes.*"

"Why? Did you read it?"

"No. But your château and your jet plane have me convinced you're a pretty good catch."

He shook his head. "Do you have any idea how long it's been since I've had a date pay for her own clothes?"

Charlotte couldn't help but smirk. "You buy your dates clothes?"

"I buy my dates many things."

"You ever stop to think you're bringing this on yourself?"

"You ever stop to think most women in the world are mercenary?"

Charlotte wasn't sure how to answer that. He was probably right. At least, he was probably right about the women he'd been hanging out with most of his life.

"Not all women are interested in your money."

The waiter stopped at their table, placing clear mugs of espresso on little blue saucers. He added a tray of sugared and chocolate-drizzled pastries in the center of the table.

The aromas hit Charlotte, reminding her that she was hungry. She pushed her arms into the sleeves of Alec's jacket and reached for a tiny cream-filled, cherry-topped morsel.

"These," she told him, "you can buy me any old time."

"That's the secret?" He chose a sugared croissant.

She nodded enthusiastically. "Pander to my sweet tooth, and I'm yours for life."

Something flickered in the depths of his brown eyes, and she instantly regretted her choice of words. They might have moved past one-night stand, but they hadn't gone anywhere beyond a fling. She was fine with that, and she didn't want Alec to worry that she had any other expectations.

She wondered if she should explain. Or would protesting just make things worse?

He considered her for a second longer. "Good to know," he said simply.

"Of course," she put into the silence, waving her pastry, "the downside is, I won't fit into the clothes for much longer."

He smiled. "I'm not worried. Your derriere's a little on the skinny side, anyway."

"Are you serious?" She twisted to look at her backside. She exercised quite extensively to keep her derriere fitting into designer clothes.

Alec laughed. "There's nothing wrong with a curve or two."

"Don't let Lesley Manichatio hear you say that."

"I already told her."

"Right."

He shrugged.

"You actually know Lesley Manichatio?"

"We carry her brands at Esmee ETA."

"Wait a minute." Charlotte set her pastry on the edge of her plate, wiping her hands on a paper napkin. "You own Esmee ETA?"

"Yes."

"The stores? The chain?"

"Uh-huh." He nodded.

"Alec?"

"Yes?"

"You really are a catch."

"You want to rethink the river cruise?"

"Not on your life."

He grinned. "At least eat your pastry."

She picked it up again.

No wonder the man was paranoid. How would he ever know if a woman fell in love with him or his money? He could write a prenup, sure. But he'd still never know. A woman could fake love for a very long time if Alec was paying the bills.

Seven

The sun slipped below the horizon, and Alec watched the lights come on up and down the Tiber River. He was in no hurry to leave the café. He didn't want to share Charlotte with Raine or anyone else just yet.

Over her empty coffee cup, she sighed at the sight. "It really is beautiful, isn't it?"

Alec reached for her hand, smoothing his thumb over her soft knuckles, moving to her palm. "Let me take you on a cruise."

She gave him a pained, wistful look.

"Don't fixate on the cost," he whispered. Then he raised her hand to his lips, turning it over to place a soft kiss on the inside of her wrist. "I want to get you alone, and I can't think of anywhere more alone than in a boat on the river."

Her glance slid to the marina below, and Alec knew he had her. He seized the opportunity, signaling the waiter. "Do you have a number for the marina?" he asked.

The man nodded and withdrew.

"I didn't say yes," Charlotte pointed out.

"Not with your lips," Alec agreed. "But you said yes with your eyes."

"That's a stretch."

He shook his head. "I've been reading women's eyes for many long years."

"Bragging?"

"Merely supporting my position."

The waiter returned with the number written on a small piece of paper, and Alec retrieved his cell phone. He made a quick call, arranged for a yacht and crew, then flipped the phone shut.

He stood from his chair and came around to hers. "We have to eat dinner somewhere," he told her.

"It's a dinner cruise?"

"It's whatever we want it to be."

The only available boat, the *Florence Maiden,* was ninety-five feet from bow to stern. She had a chef, a fully stocked galley, three luxury staterooms, a formal dining room, a hot tub on the aft deck and five crew members to ensure the entire evening ran smoothly.

Charlotte drew a deep breath. "I guess a girl's got to eat."

Alec held out his hand, helping her to her feet. "That's the spirit."

He kept her hand as they made their way down several staircases to the marina gate. There, he gave his name to a uniformed security guard.

"Berth 27B," the man informed him. "Enjoy your evening."

Still wearing his jacket, Charlotte slipped her arm into his as they moved onto the bobbing dock. It was full dark now, and the lights of Castle St. Angelo seemed even brighter across the river.

Alec noted a sign on the wharf and pointed to their left. "This way."

Charlotte turned, and they started past several dozen gleaming-white yachts berthed nose-in. "Tell me it's not the one on the end."

Alec could already see the name painted near the bow. "It's what they had available."

"You truly can't be trusted." But there wasn't a trace of anger in her tone. In fact, she sounded pleased. Well, he was feeling pretty pleased himself.

The captain greeted them at the bottom of the gangplank, welcoming them aboard. With Charlotte climbing in front of him, Alec's spirits lifted with every step upward.

They settled in padded, teak deck chairs at the bow of the boat. The steward provided a wine list, and Alec chose a merlot.

"We should call Raine."

"Why would we do that?" Alec had finally succeeded in separating Charlotte from the herd; he wasn't about to make contact.

The ship's whistle sounded and the engines rumbled as they reversed out of the berth, drawing back from the traffic, trees and buildings along the bank.

"She might be worried," said Charlotte.

"She's got my cell number. And yours, too, I imagine. She'll call if she needs anything."

"They probably expected to join us for dinner," Charlotte continued.

"They'll get over it."

The steward arrived to uncork the wine. He offered Alec a taste and, at Alec's nod, filled their glasses.

"The chef can offer you a seven-course Italian dinner, featuring *gamberi al Limone* and *rigatoni alla Caruso*. If you prefer French, he has a lovely *petits tournedos aux poivres vert* accompanied by *la salade du Montmartre*. Or he can prepare a grilled filet mignon, Portobello mushrooms, with a traditional Caesar salad."

Alec looked to Charlotte. "When in Rome?"

"The Italian dinner sounds perfect," she said to the steward.

As the man walked away, she leaned closer to Alec. "We can only hope the pasta will improve the size of my derriere."

Alec leaned toward her, keeping his voice at a con-spiratorial level. "I'll let you know later."

"Feeling pretty sure of yourself?"

He glanced at the moon, the water, the lights of the city and Charlotte wrapped in his jacket lounging back amongst the subtle lights of the yacht's deck. "So far, so good," he admitted, taking a satisfied sip of the merlot.

"It is nice to get away from the crowds," Charlotte agreed. "The noise."

"The explosions."

"Sorry about that."

"Did you see your father this morning?" asked Alec.

She shook her head.

"He was due in, right?"

Her gaze went to a cloud wisping across the moon. "Yes, he was."

"But you didn't stay to say hello?"

She watched straight over the bow. "I didn't want to hold everybody up."

Alec considered her profile for a moment. "You didn't want to see him," he concluded.

"I told you, it's not the same as Jack. With David, I don't care one way or the other."

"What about the rest of the family?"

"What about them?"

"Your cousins Dev and Max were coming in today. And Isabella would have been on set. Don't you want to get to know them?"

Charlotte's expression tightened.

"You escaped, didn't you?" Alec guessed.

She waved a dismissive hand. "I needed clothes."

"You could have had some shipped from home."

She mustered a cocky grin. "And where would be the fun in that?"

"Charlotte," Alec pressed. "Are you afraid of your family?"

"It's not the same as for you."

"Blood is still blood," said Alec. He had dozens of aunts, uncles, cousins and second cousins in and around Provence. Montcalm family occasions were large, boisterous and entertaining. It didn't matter how seldom he saw some relatives, they always meant something.

She gathered his jacket closer around her.

"You said you missed Jack," Alec pointed out, struggling to figure out her feelings. "Now's your chance to get to know him."

Storm clouds gathered behind her blue eyes. "It's complicated."

"That's just part of the package. You want to hear about my Uncle Rudy and his affair with cousin Giselle's next-door neighbor? Or the time Uncle Bovier disinherited his eldest son, Leroy, because he was gay? Talk about a crisis. My phone rang off the hook for weeks." Alec took a breath.

"At least you know them," said Charlotte.

"Not that well." There were members of his family he saw only once a year.

"And." She gave a hollow laugh. "They didn't give you away."

Alec stilled.

Her voice went hard. "Nobody looked at you and Raine, and said, 'We like Raine better. Give Alec away.'"

"I'm sure it wasn't—"

"I have one father, an aunt and uncle, two grand-parents, a brother and four cousins on the Hudson side of the family, and not one, not *one of them* thought I was worth keeping." She closed her eyes, shook her head and took a swallow of her wine.

"I was wrong," Alec put in softly, drinking in the intense emotion on her face. "You're not scared. You're angry." He nodded to himself. "That makes sense. You have every right to be angry with them."

She waved her glass for emphasis. "My grandparents took wonderful care of me."

"You waited your whole life for Jack to come and rescue you. He never did."

"Jack was a little boy."

"Emotions have nothing to do with logic." Alec rose from his chair, crossing the polished, redwood deck. He crouched next to Charlotte's chair. "If you could control your emotions with logic, would you be here?"

She gazed silently into his eyes.

"It's a risk, you and me. For you, it's your reputation. For me..." He gave a short laugh. "Well, all the usual reasons. Plus, you're Raine's friend, and she's going to kill me if you get hurt."

"I'm not going to get hurt."

"I'm counting on that," Alec said honestly. He might be narcissistic and self-centered, but he didn't deliberately set out to hurt anyone. He tried hard to choose independent, worldly women. That they were mostly gold diggers was regrettable, but then the breakup disappointed them on more of a financial level than an emotional one. And that was good.

He heard the steward behind him with the first course.

Alec came to his feet. He'd hold Charlotte in his arms later and try to chase away her demons. It was a temporary fix for both of them, but it was all they had.

The water in the aft-deck hot tub swirled around Charlotte's naked body. Soft, underwater lighting reflected on the blue walls, highlighting her pale skin and Alec's arms where they wrapped around her waist to anchor across her stomach.

Angry at the Hudsons? At first she'd dismissed Alec's theory. Schooled by her diplomat grandfather and gentle, compassionate grandmother, Charlotte always had her emotions completely under control. She wasn't given to outbursts of anger. She was analytical and empathetic. Anger was a self-indulgent emotion that was never productive.

But as dinner moved on, something pricked at her brain: Could Alec could be right? Had she spent the past twenty-one years repressing her anger? Was that why her stomach churned at the thought of seeing the Hudsons?

She'd always felt like an outsider. And she'd long since admitted to her jealousy of her cousins and their easy familiarity with each other. But was there more?

"Stop thinking," Alec rumbled in her ear, giving her a quick kiss on the temple, his arms tightening for a split second around her waist.

She was cradled in his lap beneath the warm water. He'd asked the ship staff to give them privacy, so they were alone on the dark deck, surrounded by a smoked-glass guardrail. Clouds had been moving in for an hour, and the city lights turned blurry as the first rain-drops plunked into the tub.

Charlotte snuggled against the cocoon of Alec's body. She didn't feel like an outsider now. In fact, for the first time in her life, she was at the center of the universe—hers and Alec's. She recognized the danger of those feelings and vowed they wouldn't get out of control. But for now, for tonight, Alec was a welcome break from the reality she'd have to face back at the movie set.

The rain grew heavy, fat droplets splashing into the hot tub.

"You want to go inside?" asked Alec.

"I like it here," she responded, reluctant to break the spell.

"I like it, too." He kissed her neck, tracing a trail to her damp shoulder and back again.

"You taste good."

"It's the rainwater."

"No, it's not."

She tipped her head to one side, giving him freer access. His large hands slipped up her stomach, covering her breasts. "You're soft," he muttered. "So soft."

She dropped her head right back, and he placed a warm, wet kiss on her lips.

"Have you stopped thinking?" he asked.

"I think you're magic," she answered, and he smiled.

"It's nice to be magic."

He kissed her again, more seriously this time. Then he carefully turned her so she was facing him, straddling his lap, her arms loosely around his neck.

He shimmied her close. "Do you want anything?"

"Besides you?"

"Coffee, brandy, dessert?"

"You're going to call the steward?" She glanced meaningfully down at their naked bodies.

"We can have it delivered to the stateroom."

"I assumed you had something else in mind for the stateroom."

He smoothed back her wet hair. "I'm in no rush."

Then his expression turned serious. "We've got all night."

"What about Rai—"

He put an index finger across her lips. "Nobody's called. Nobody's going to call. It's just you and me." His gaze trailed from her neck to her breasts, her stomach and below. "You are astonishingly beautiful. I could sit here and stare at you all night."

"That's only because you can't see my skinny derriere."

"Turn around."

"I don't believe I will."

"I've grown fond of your derriere." He slipped a hand beneath her and gave a squeeze. "Plus, you ate all that pasta."

She struggled not to wriggle under his hand. But it was strong and warm and oh-so-sensual. "The pasta was delicious."

Alec kissed her mouth. "A dismal second."

"To?"

He drew back. "You fishing for more compliments?"

"Oh." She pretended to suddenly understand. "A dismal second to *me*."

He chuckled low. "You are shameless."

She gave in, shifting her body so that his hand touched the sensitive spot between her legs.

"Pretty much," she agreed in a husky voice.

His eyes darkened, and he leaned in for a very serious kiss, his fingertips setting out on an exploration that made her gasp, even as cool rain water trickled down her spine.

"Inside?" he rasped, and she quickly nodded her agreement.

He lifted her out of the tub, wrapped them both in thick, white robes and carried her the short distance to the master stateroom.

The room was huge, with a cushioned, cream-colored carpet, gleaming cherrywood paneling, a massive bed with a rose-colored comforter, eight pillows and a padded bench at the foot. There were mirrors on the ceiling, oil paintings on the walls and a subtly textured, cream wallpaper that wrapped around a sitting nook with overstuffed furniture and porcelain lamps. Several flower arrangements gave the room a sweet, subtle scent.

Alec set her down on the soft carpet, dragging back the comforter to reveal crisp, white sheets. He tossed most of the pillows, then tugged at the sash of her robe. With warm hands, he brushed the terry-cloth from her shoulders, easing the fabric down her arms, until it cascaded to a pool at her feet.

"Amazing," he whispered, drawing back to gaze at her naked body.

Charlotte felt amazing. She loved the warm look in his eyes, the hiss of his indrawn breath, the power of his muscled body as he tossed his own robe and stood naked before her.

She reached out to touch his chest, his skin warm under her fingertips. "Amazing," she echoed.

He stepped forward. His palm cupped the curve of her hip, drawing her in. His other hand touched her chin, tipping her face ever so gently as he bent toward her for a soft kiss.

"I don't want tonight to end," he told her.

Neither did she. "What if we keep sailing? Into the Mediterranean, through the Strait of Gibraltar and out into the Pacific."

"Don't tempt me."

"They'd probably send a search party."

He raised an eyebrow. "But I wonder how many times we could make love before they found us?"

"I wonder how many times we can make love tonight?" she countered.

"Now there's a challenge." He backed her into the edge of the bed, kissed her soundly, his hands roaming, while she gave up any pretense at control, dragging him onto the bed, kissing his mouth, tasting his skin, running her hands down his back, his thighs, kneading his hard muscles, before sitting up to straddle his body.

They both groaned at the contact, staring into each other's eyes. His hands bracketed her hips, easing inside her. He was huge and hot, and she gasped as sparks spread out to touch her fingers and her toes.

He locked his hands with hers, and he flexed his hips. She matched him thrust for thrust, her head tipping back, and the world sliding into a cataclysm of color until she cried out his name and he wrapped her in an engulfing hug.

Hours later, they lay side by side, he on his back, she sprawled on her stomach. She felt as though she might never move again.

Through bleary eyes, she watched him liberate a long-stemmed rose from the vase beside the bed. He stroked its soft petals along her shoulder, down the indent of her waist, over the curve of her hip then across her derriere.

"I've changed my mind," he said, "your derriere is perfect."

She couldn't help but smile. "You do know how to show a girl a good time."

"I try."

"You didn't have to do all this," she continued. The yacht, the hot tub, the amazing dinner. "I'd have slept with you again anyway."

His voice was a low rumble. "You mean I could have checked us into the Plaza Della Famiglia for thirty euro and had my way with you?"

She smiled. "Yes," she answered honestly.

He stared, not moving, at the ceiling for a while.

There was a funny catch to his voice when he spoke

again. "That means a lot to me." He paused. "Knowing that you mean it."

Then he rose on his elbow to gaze down at her. "But it's also important to me that I didn't do that."

She nodded, understanding, touched by his point. And, quite frankly, a luxury yacht made for better memories than a cheap motel.

He gently brushed a lock of hair back from her cheek. "Of all the women…" He went silent for a long minute. Then he leaned forward to kiss her mouth.

He pulled her almost fiercely to him, kissing harder and deeper. Her energy returned in a rush, and their naked bodies meshed together. The rain drummed steadily on the window and lightning flashed in the sky, while the yacht, droning steadily, made a lazy turn to head back up the Tiber River.

They made it to the airport just in time to greet Raine and Kiefer and jump on the jet to get to London. The Montcalm Gulfstream had two seating areas, four armchairs facing each other at the front of the cabin and a couch, table and two side-facing armchairs at the back.

Raine seemed uncomfortable as they boarded, moving to the back and buckling in on the white leather couch. Charlotte followed, wondering if she'd somehow offended her friend by staying out all night. She and Raine were sharing a hotel suite, so Raine had to be fully aware that Charlotte had spent the night with Alec.

Alec and Kiefer sat down in the second row, on opposite sides of the aisle, facing forward. The captain came back to talk to Alec, while a steward offered drinks all around. Charlotte said yes to champagne and orange juice, steeling her courage to face Raine.

"You all right?" she asked Raine as the jet taxied for takeoff. Alec and Kiefer had immediately settled in to a work discussion.

"Yeah." Raine nodded without glancing Charlotte's way.

"The meeting?" Charlotte forced herself to ask. "It went well?"

Raine gave another nod.

The engines whined to full throttle, the jet gaining speed before smoothly lifting off the runway, climbing fast and banking north.

As they leveled, and the noise subsided, Charlotte gathered her courage. "Raine, I have to—"

"You're probably wondering," Raine interrupted, glancing worriedly at the two men in the front of the cabin. She leaned close to Charlotte. "You're probably wondering why I didn't show up last night."

Charlotte was confused. "Show up?"

Raine nodded. "At the hotel. I—" Her eyes darted to Alec for a split second. "I was with Kiefer."

Charlotte raised a hand to her lips to cover up the smile. "You spent the night with Kiefer?"

Raine nodded, looking pained. "I wasn't going to—" She twisted her hands around her clutch purse. "I know I said I wouldn't—"

"I slept with Alec," Charlotte admitted in an effort to lessen Raine's embarrassment.

Raine drew back. "Huh?"

"I didn't go back to the hotel suite, either."

"You slept with Alec?" Raine hissed.

"Shh." Charlotte checked out the backs of the men's heads to make sure they weren't listening. "Yes."

"So you didn't even *know* I wasn't there?"

"Didn't have a clue," said Charlotte.

"I could have gotten away with it?"

Charlotte nodded. "But you *slept* with Kiefer? What happened?"

"After the meeting," said Raine, keeping her voice down, "we went to dinner. I wondered why you guys didn't call, by the way."

"I wondered why you didn't call us."

"There was dancing," said Raine. "And, well…"

"He now knows you think he's hot?" Charlotte suggested.

"He knows now."

Both women stared ahead in silence for a moment.

"And Alec?" asked Raine.

"Knows I think he's hot, too."

Raine nodded, a grin growing rapidly on her face.

Suddenly, both women burst out laughing.

The two men turned to stare.

"Nothing," Raine assured them.

"Girl talk," said Charlotte.

Alec's eyes narrowed in suspicion, but Charlotte gave him a benign shrug. It wasn't her place to give away secrets. After a minute, the men went back to their conversation.

"What now?" asked Raine.

Charlotte didn't know how to answer that. Last night had been magic, from shopping to coffee to the yacht. But in the cold light of day, she had no idea what Alec would expect.

"What now for you?" she asked Raine, stalling for time.

"Honestly? I think it's going to get really awkward, really fast," said Raine. "It was great, but now we have to work together." She folded her arms over her chest and leaned her head back on the seat. "There's just no way this ends well."

Charlotte nodded, understanding completely. *Really awkward, really fast,* was a good way to put it. It was some consolation that she'd be done with the movie in a few weeks. After that, she and Alec's paths didn't need to cross. But for Raine, a fling with Kiefer was a whole lot more complicated. She wished she had some helpful advice to offer. But she had nothing.

Alec rose from his seat and moved down the aisle, his expression serious. He nodded to Raine. "Kiefer would like to talk to you."

Without meeting her brother's eyes, Raine scrambled to her feet and moved up the cabin.

Alec stayed behind, taking the seat next to Charlotte. And when he turned to her, his expression softened.

"Hey." He smiled.

"Hey." Despite the circumstances, she couldn't help but smile back.

"How are you feeling?"

"I'm fine."

"Tired?"

"A little."

Between their bodies, he took her hand in his. "So, what do you want to do in London?"

She didn't want to be presumptuous. Though she'd happily spend more time with him. "What do *you* want to do in London?" She put it back on him.

Unexpectedly, he cupped her cheek, raking spread fingers back into her loose hair, pulling her forward for a kiss.

"Kiefer," she warned in an undertone, as Alec's lips closed over hers.

"Kiefer knows," said Alec against her mouth. Then he kissed her deeply. *"This* is what I want to do in London."

"For two whole days?"

"Yes."

"Did Kiefer say…anything?" Charlotte asked carefully.

Alec nodded toward the front of the cabin. "Take a look."

She twisted her head to see Raine sitting across Kiefer's lap in the big armchair. They were whispering and giggling together.

"I feel like I'm in high school," she told Alec.

He agreed with a nod. "But with much better transportation and a platinum card."

"You're going to try to spend money on me in London, aren't you?"

"Try?" he scoffed, cocking his head and giving her a smirk. "I've already booked a suite at the Ritz and a box on the Grand Tier at Covent Garden."

Eight

By the time they made it through London and Paris, Charlotte felt like a spoiled princess. She'd given up arguing with Alec about money. She even gave up trying to pay for her own clothes. He'd simply worn her down.

But now they were back in Provence. One of Alec's drivers had delivered the Lamborghini to the airport. So they'd stowed the luggage in the limo with Raine and Kiefer and were speeding under the streetlights, top down, along the highway with jazz pouring out of the sound system. She'd dressed casually for the trip, in a new pair of designer jeans and a cropped, peach tank top with flat lace insets.

Alec was a steady, confident driver. And as their speed increased, she kicked off her sandals and tipped her head back, letting the cool wind flow over her skin.

"Almost home," said Alec, shifting out of Sixth as the turnoff to Château Montcalm came into view.

She tried to formulate the right sentiment. She watched Alec's profile as the aspen and oak trees flashed by.

"What?" He glanced over.

Straightforward seemed like the best choice. "I had a really great time, Alec."

He grinned. "Me, too."

Their gazes caught and held.

"Thank you," she told him sincerely.

"Anytime," he breathed, turning his attention back to the road, slowing down further as the château's driveway loomed.

Charlotte let out a sigh, sliding her feet back into her sandals. As the headlights caught the semitrailers, the scarred lawn and the open-air buffet tables that provided craft services to the crew during the day, she tried to smooth her hair into some sort of order. But she quickly gave up. And when Alec brought the convertible to a halt at the front door, she decided a shower would be first on her list. She might as well get rid of the dust along with the tangles.

Alec swung around to open her door, and Charlotte came to her feet, stretching out her neck and back after the long journey. The film set was quiet as they crossed to the front door, with just a few grips, production assistants and security guards putting things in place for the morning.

Alec pushed open the wide door, and the quiet of the yard disappeared. Chitchat and music wafted out from the great room. Several people laughed, while Lars's unmistakable voice proposed a toast to Isabella.

Charlotte's stomach clenched in alarm. The Hudsons wouldn't, they would *not* hold a party in Alec's château while he was away. She cautiously glanced up at him. His mouth was set in a firm line, and before she could even register the anger in his eyes, he was marching toward the archway leading to the great room.

Though Charlotte dreaded what she'd find, she felt compelled to follow along.

"Monsieur Montcalm?" Henri hustled out from the hallway to ambush Alec.

"Not now, Henri," Alec growled, brushing past.

"But, *monsieur.*"

"Save it." Alec kept walking. It was the first time she'd ever heard him utter a sharp word to a member of his staff, certainly not to Henri.

"Madame Lillian Hudson arrived this afternoon."

Alec didn't react, but Charlotte certainly did. Lillian was here? Her grandmother had shown up on the set?

"Given her age and *illness,*" Henri stressed, striding along beside Alec, "I thought it wise to invite her to stay in the château."

Alec's steps faltered.

"I was certain, were you here, you would insist," said Henri, a wealth of meaning in his tone.

"She's ill?" Alec asked, a muscle twitching near his left eye.

"She has cancer," Charlotte supplied in a pained voice. They'd done it. Her family had actually thrown a party in Alec's home.

"I put her in the Bombay room with her son, Markus, next door. The rest of the family is with Jack at the hotel."

Alec's nostrils flared as he sucked in a sharp breath.

"I'm so sorry," Charlotte whispered.

Alec glanced at her, but said nothing.

Henri's voice went to an undertone. "Dinner tonight is to welcome Lillian to Provence."

Alec was silent a second longer. But then he gave a sharp nod. "Thank you, Henri."

Henri nodded in return. "Of course, *monsieur.*"

Then Alec held out his arm to Charlotte. "Will you introduce me to your family?"

Charlotte's stomach clenched tighter. Judging by the noise level, the entire family, along with assorted production staff, were in Alec's great room. She was tired, trail weary, dusty and disheveled. She didn't want to see the Hudsons or anyone else right now.

But she couldn't say no to Alec. He'd been extraordinarily patient under some very trying circumstances. So, instead of protesting, she nodded and took his arm. They walked through the archway to the stone-walled, high-ceilinged great room. Its polished hardwood floors, Aubusson rugs and Louis XV furnishings were covered in wall-to-wall Hudsons— Charlotte's grandmother Lillian, her uncle Markus, her father, David, her brother, Jack, and cousins Dev and Max, and Isabella chatting intimately with Ridley Sinclair.

Jack was the first person to notice Alec. As he came forward, Charlotte quickly disentangled herself from Alec's arm.

"Alec," Jack stated heartily, extending his hand. "Great to have you back."

"Thank you," Alec intoned, but Charlotte could hear the tension in his voice.

Jack turned. "Everybody, this is Alec Montcalm, our host."

There was a chorus of greetings and a surge forward that halted when people realized Lillian was making her way to Alec.

Everyone, including Alec, waited as the frail-looking woman approached him.

"Mr. Montcalm," came Lillian's steady voice.

Alec took a few steps forward to close the distance.

"Mrs. Hudson," he nodded, gently taking her hand between his. "A pleasure to meet you at last."

"My thanks, on behalf of my entire family, for your hospitality."

"No thanks are necessary," said Alec. "It is my pleasure."

No one listening could have guessed at the trials and tribulations Alec had been through with the film so far.

Charlotte's glance caught Jack's, and when his gaze slid along her outfit, she remembered her appearance. If only the archway or even the patio door were a little closer, she'd slip out. But the last thing she wanted to do was call attention to herself.

"As you may know," said Lillian, "this film is near and dear to my heart."

Alec stood to one side and gestured to Charlotte. "Your granddaughter expressed that quite eloquently."

Lillian and the entire family turned their attention to Charlotte.

Charlotte's hand went reflexively to her messy hair. Then she wondered if dust was smudged on her cheeks or if every wrinkle in her clothing was visible under the great room lights.

"Hello, Lillian," she managed.

"Lovely to see you, dear." Lillian nodded regally.

"It was Charlotte who convinced me to allow Hudson Pictures to use my château," Alec continued.

Charlotte could see what Alec was trying to do, and it was admirable. But she could also see he was making Markus uncomfortable. It was his project, and he didn't seem used to other people taking the spotlight.

Sure enough, Markus stepped forward. "Markus Hudson." He offered his hand to Alec and shook heartily. "CEO of Hudson Pictures."

With everyone's attention on Alec and Markus, Charlotte took a step backward. She was escaping to the shower just as soon as humanly possible. She could always come back for a drink later and say her hellos. Hopefully, by then, her new clothes would have arrived in the limo. They would boost her confidence.

While Alec and Markus talked, she eased carefully backward.

But then Jack appeared by her side. "I hear you were in London," he opened.

Charlotte gave another hopeless swipe at her hair before answering. "And Rome and Paris."

Jack nodded, a glance straying to Alec.

"Raine wanted to go shopping," Charlotte quickly put in. "You met Raine, right? It was mostly her who helped me convince Alec to let you film here. She should be right behind us." Charlotte glanced toward the hall. "With Kiefer, the vice president of Montcalm."

"You okay?" Jack wedged in.

"Fine." Charlotte clamped her mouth shut.

Jack nodded across the room at their father. "You going to say hello?"

"I'm not in a rush." If she could avoid it, she would. Her emotional state was better if she simply avoided her father altogether.

At the moment, David was working on a martini—no surprise there. He was also watching his brother, Markus, through squinting eyes, his lips pursed in obvious annoyance. She knew the two brothers didn't get along. She might be out of touch, but that much family gossip had come her way.

Again, no surprise. David might be a talented director, but he was also narcissistic and egotistical. And from what she'd been able to glean, Markus had little patience for difficult personalities.

"Show him you're not intimidated," Jack suggested.

"I'm not," she lied. She was intimidated by the entire family, particularly en masse. And she knew talking to David would have the power to zap her back to the unwanted little girl at the airport.

"Glad to hear it," said Jack, taking a sip from his crystal tumbler. Then there was a sneer in his voice. "Because he's definitely not worth it."

Charlotte simply nodded.

"You will say hello to Cece, right?" Jack referred to his new wife.

"After I shower," Charlotte agreed. "I really need to get cleaned up."

"Theo's a great kid," Jack put in, voice softening as he gazed across the room once again. "And I'm going to be a wonderful father. And that man…" The hard voice came back in force. "That man will *not* influence me in any way. I am not him."

Charlotte felt an instant admiration for her brother. He'd obviously come to terms with his childhood. She was happy for him, but she couldn't help but feel even more lonely.

"I won't let him define me," Jack finished.

Charlotte wished she could be that strong. But she was a long way from not letting her upbringing define her.

Alec was right when he said she was angry. But she was also hurt. And she was also lonely. And being around the Hudsons, especially David, made her wonder if anybody in the world would ever choose her, ever truly love her, just for herself.

Alec saw Charlotte leave the great room. His initial reaction was to go after her, but Markus was still talking, and he was curious about her father, who was sitting off to one side, looking sullen as he watched his older brother through narrowed eyes.

Lillian had said good-night, and was being helped back to her room. Alec had been introduced to Isabella and Ridley Sinclair. Judging by their expressions and body language, he'd bet the affair rumors were true. He wondered if he should alert Kiefer. It wasn't too late to sneak a tabloid reporter onto the property, or give them a heads-up on the location of the stars' villa rental.

Markus had also introduced his sons Dev and Max. Both seemed hardworking and intelligent. Dev was planning to leave with his father and Lillian within the next few days. Max planned to stay to work with David on a daily basis. It was easy to see there was no love lost between Markus's side of the family and his brother, David.

In fact, Alec wondered why David was directing the film at all, until he overheard Isabella comment on

David's artistic and dramatic vision. Apparently, vision was a difficult thing to come by in Hollywood. That would explain why everyone put up with Lars's temperamental nature. Alec would have fired the man weeks ago.

At a lull in the conversation, Alec excused himself and approached David.

"Alec Montcalm." He offered his hand.

David had the grace to stand up from the armchair in front of the stone fireplace. "David Hudson."

"I understand you're directing the film?"

"Is that all you understand?" David's gaze slid to Markus; he was obviously wondering if his brother had been badmouthing him to Alec.

"Can I freshen your drink?" asked Alec, nodding to the near-empty glass.

David glanced down. "It's the Glen Klavit. One ice cube."

Alec gave a brief nod to a staff member, and indicated David's glass. "I'll have the same," he told the waiter.

"A man with good taste in scotch," David commented.

"I visited Klavit Castle last year," Alec said conversationally. "Almost inaccessible, and damn cold. But there's no better place on earth for distilling coastal whiskey."

David nodded as the waiter presented their drinks on a silver tray.

"Charlotte and I were in London last week." As a segue, it was a stretch, but Alec didn't want to be at this all night.

"I was wandering through your pool house," said David, as if his daughter's name hadn't even been mentioned. "And I was wondering, would you be open to a minor renovation?"

"We stayed at the Ritz," said Alec. "Took in the Royal Ballet."

David's eyes narrowed, as if he was assessing Alec's mental competence. "Uh, right. Always a treat. There's a lighting problem with the pool house. We'd like to add a window in the front. When we pan left, we're going to lose the natural light on Isabella, and the mood can't be too somber. It's the pivotal scene where Lillian and Charles pledge their love. I thought about backlighting." David's eyes lost focus. "But we're going for realism, not some overly romanticized—"

"As long as you don't use explosives," Alec cut in.

David drew back with a frown, obviously missing the joke. "It's a love scene."

"I see."

"It's midway thought the script. The conflicts have been well set up, and the central characters are—"

"Sure," said Alec, taking a bracing swig of the scotch, wishing he'd gone for something that was cask strength. "Put in a window."

"That's good," said David with a distracted nod. "Then I can talk to wardrobe about Lillian's hat."

"Whatever," said Alec, realizing Charlotte had nothing in common with her father.

He glanced across the room to where Jack was talking with his cousin Max. David and Jack both had dark hair and blue eyes. But there was nothing definitively similar about their appearances, either.

"We might need a few extra shooting days," David put in. "I have Cece working on script revisions."

"No problem," said Alec. As long as Charlotte stuck around with them, the film crew could stay here as long as they liked.

Charlotte had missed breakfast. Exhausted from lack of sleep in Rome, London and Paris, and battling butterflies in her stomach at the proximity of all those Hudsons, she'd buried her face under the covers and dozed until nearly ten.

The house was quiet as she wandered into the kitchen, the noise from the film set filtered by the thick stone walls. Cece was in the breakfast nook, script pages spread out in front of her, with her two-year-old son, Theo, playing trains on the floor. Cece had recently revealed the fact that Theo was Jack's son, making him Charlotte's nephew.

For some reason, Cece and Theo weren't nearly as intimidating as the rest of the clan. Maybe it was because they were new to the family.

"Good morning," Charlotte offered, pouring herself a cup of coffee from the big island counter.

"Morning," Cece returned with a smile, her brown hair flowing softly around her delicate face, coffee-toned eyes warm and welcoming.

Charlotte immediately relaxed, her stomach calming down for the first time in hours. "Am I disturbing you?"

Cece shook her head. "David's being a jerk this morning. He can damn well wait for the new pages."

Then she seemed to remember who Charlotte was. Her face flushed slightly. "Oops. Sorry."

"For insulting the man who abandoned me and made my mother's life a living hell?" Charlotte plunked down on the bench seat across from Cece. "Wow. Don't know where that came from."

"It was well earned. I hope it was cathartic."

"I take it you and Jack have discussed our *father?*"

"Jack and I have discussed quite a lot of things in the past couple of months."

Charlotte was hit with an unwelcome pang of jealousy. She squelched it. "I'm glad you found each other," she said in all honesty. "And I'm sorry I missed the wedding."

"It was very short notice," Cece allowed.

"We were in China," Charlotte explained. "I couldn't leave the ambassador."

"Jack told me." Her attention suddenly shifted. "Not in your mouth, sweetheart."

Charlotte glanced down at Theo. His cherubic little face was scrunched up in a grin as he gnawed on a section of wooden train track.

"He's adorable," she told Cece.

"He looks just like his father," said Cece, and Charlotte's eyes suddenly burned.

She quickly blinked, raising her coffee for a sip to cover up. "Are you thinking about brothers or sisters?"

Cece smiled. "You bet. We're a little behind on timing, but we're planning to make it up in effort."

Charlotte laughed. Jack's children, growing up in a stable, loving home. It was a wonderful turn of events.

Two figures passed by the window outside. It was Max and his assistant, Dana Fallon.

"They're moving around back today. Shots in the garden, I think," said Cece.

Max shouted a question across the lawn to the assistant director. The man answered with hand gestures.

Dana started to say something, but Max strode away.

Charlotte caught an unguarded look of longing on Dana's face.

"Oh, dear," she whispered under her breath, cradling her warm, stoneware cup.

"I know," said Cece. "She's got it bad for Max."

"Does he know?"

Cece shook her head. "The man is oblivious to everything but work. And she's such a great girl."

"Should somebody clue him in? Maybe Jack?"

Cece raised her brow. "If you were her, would you want somebody to clue the guy in?"

Charlotte couldn't help thinking about her growing feelings for Alec. Alec was a playboy, a womanizer; he didn't have the slightest interest in a serious relationship. Would she want some helpful soul telling him that she was falling for him?

Not on your life. As long as she kept her secret, she could have a few more weeks of paradise. The second it was out, he would run for the hills.

"No," she admitted. "I suppose Dana's best chance is if Max notices himself. You suppose there's anything we can do to help that happen?"

Cece gave a sly grin, and Charlotte felt her first true connection with a member of the Hudson family.

"Morning, all," came Raine's sleepy voice.

"Hi, Raine," Charlotte answered. "Have you met Cece? She's the screenwriter and my new sister-in-law." The title felt odd on Charlotte's tongue, but she forced herself to use it anyway.

"We haven't met," said Raine, holding out a hand to shake.

"You have a lovely home," said Cece. "It's going to give the picture such authenticity."

"I only hope it's standing when you're done," said Raine, pouring herself some coffee and selecting a pastry, before hopping up on one of the bar stools at the island counter.

"I heard about the explosion," said Cece. "And I saw the aftermath. You do know they'll pay for it."

"As long as no one was hurt," said Raine, taking a big bite of the beignet.

Cece glanced down at the script pages. "I'm trying to keep the rest of the battle scenes to a minimum."

"We appreciate that," said Charlotte.

"But you have to admit," Raine put in, "it was exciting."

"It was definitely exciting," Charlotte agreed. As had been the preceding hours in Alec's bed. That was the first time they'd made love. It was fantastic, and it had actually improved with time.

Not that his technique had needed one iota of improvement. But she knew him better now, knew him and liked him. Liked him a lot.

Oh, no.

This was bad.

"I think I'll go change," she told the other two women, coming to her feet.

A sudden wave of dizziness flashed through her brain, and she grabbed the edge of the table to steady herself.

"Too many sleepless nights?" Raine teased.

And Cece's interest perked.

"Parties in London and Paris," Charlotte quickly explained, resisting the urge to glare at Raine. "I slept great last night."

"We're not as young as we used to be," Cece chimed in.

"Speak for yourself," said Raine. "I can still party like a nineteen-year-old."

"Not if you want your circulation numbers back up," came Kiefer's voice. He gave Raine a mock stern look as he entered the room.

Then something passed between them, something strong and intimate that made Charlotte jealous. Which was silly. If Raine and Kiefer were happy together, it was nothing but good news. And if Jack and Cece had found joy together, Charlotte was thrilled for them.

Still, an indefinable emotion clogged her throat, and she mumbled something more about getting dressed, then she quickly left the kitchen. Alec had been too nice to her the past few days. She was beginning to read things into it that simply weren't there. He was a decent guy who had a lot of experience in dating. He also had an unlimited credit card, which helped him entertain in style.

She had to stop confusing his innate class and hospitality for deeper feelings.

Nine

Two days later, Lillian, Markus and Dev, along with Dev's fiancée, Valerie Shelton, left Provence. Alec finally felt as if he had a little privacy. He waited until after midnight, until the set was quiet and the staff had retired for the night. Dressed in a pair of jogging shorts and a simple T-shirt, he padded down the hallway to Charlotte's room.

He silently cracked open her door. Moonlight shone through the billowing sheer curtains, reflecting off her soft skin and blond hair. Her covers were half off in the warm evening, revealing the lace-inset, purple silk nightgown she'd bought in Rome.

He'd wanted to buy it for her. He still wished he'd bought it for her. He wanted to feel some ownership of the garment. And, he admitted to himself, he wanted to feel some ownership of the woman wearing it.

It was a ridiculous and inappropriate emotion. Charlotte didn't need him in her life. Everything she'd said and done for the past three weeks told him she wanted stability. She wanted family. She wanted a man she could count on.

Nobody could count on Alec.

Still, it didn't stop him from wanting her.

He crossed the room, crouching down beside the big bed.

"Charlotte?" he whispered.

She stirred in her sleep.

He brushed a hand gently over her hair. "Charlotte?"

She groaned. "Did they catch the château on fire?"

He smiled. "No. Everything's still standing. You asleep?"

"I was." She blinked her eyes open in the dappled light.

"I was lonely," he confessed.

After a silent moment, she smiled sweetly up at him. "Me, too."

"Thank goodness."

She slid over, and he slipped into the bed beside her.

He wrapped an arm around her waist and pulled her backward against his body. "I like you in silk." He nuzzled against her neck, kissing her hairline, breathing in the intoxicating scent of her skin. "I like you out of silk, too." He slipped his hand below the hem of the short nightgown, sliding it up to her flat belly, letting it rest against the softness.

Then he kissed the side of her neck, drawing her earlobe into his mouth.

"Are we sleeping or making love?" she asked.

"Do you have a preference?" He did. But he was

willing to compromise anything if it meant he could hold her in his arms tonight.

"Just getting clarification."

"Any reason we can't do both?"

"I've been having a little trouble getting up in the mornings."

"I can be quick," he offered. "And then you can get right to sleep."

He felt her body quiver with laughter. "Such a gentleman."

He moved his hand to the curve of her breast. "Does fast work for you?"

She turned onto her back, and he could just make out her expression in the moonlight. She was such an incredibly beautiful woman, and his heart did a funny flip-flop as he gazed into her eyes.

"Slow works for me," she told him, slipping her small, soft fingertips under the hem of his T-shirt and stretching it off over his head.

"Slow it is." He leaned in for a full-on kiss.

Her warm lips softened and parted. He was instantly lost in their magic. A cool breeze danced over his bare back, while his blood heated to a boil. But still he kissed her, holding her close, worshipping her body, moving ever so slowly, ever so patiently into more intimate kisses, more intimate caresses, making love to her until they both collapsed from exhaustion.

Even then, he held her close. Less than half-awake, at the first streaks of dawn, he longed for things he knew could never be.

Charlotte woke up alone. It was late, and the film set below on the front lawn was a hive of activity.

Equipment was humming. People were shouting. And the greasy smells from the catering-truck breakfast grill permeated her bedroom.

Her stomach roiled.

She jumped out of bed and rushed to the bathroom, vomiting briefly into the toilet.

She sat back on the cool tiles, rubbing a sheen of sweat from her forehead. No matter how amazing it was with Alec in the middle of the night, she had to start getting some sleep. Raine might feel like a teenager, but Charlotte's system was clearly rebelling.

She rose shakily to her feet, splashing water on her face and brushing her teeth at the sink. Now that the dizzy spell had passed, she was hungry. Really hungry.

Maybe she'd grab a snack first, then get a shower later. She reached for the robe hanging on the back of the bathroom door.

Suddenly, she froze.

She was incredibly hungry, and not the least bit ill.

This was four mornings now that she'd felt temporarily nauseated.

She did some quick math in her head, then she dropped weakly to sit on the edge of the tub.

No.

It couldn't be.

They'd used a condom, and the odds against it were astronomical.

Still.

She cringed and dropped her face into her palms.

Her period was five days late, and she'd just vomited at the smell of bacon.

She had to get her hands on a home pregnancy test.

* * *

Positive.

Charlotte stared at the parallel magenta lines on the little plastic wand. She was pregnant. She was going to have Alec Montcalm's baby, angering him and disgracing her grandfather all in one fell swoop. Alec hadn't signed up for this.

And what would the Hudsons think? They'd realize she'd been carrying on an affair right here under their noses. Any respect she'd hoped to gain from Jack was gone. And Lillian. Lillian was from another time, another age. Charlotte barely knew her grandmother, and *this* was what Lillian would learn about her. Especially after learning of her brother Jack's wife Cece's pregnancy. She kept that a secret from Jack for two years. How would Lillian cope in another scandal?

She swiped at a wayward tear.

She was pregnant.

She had to be strong.

There was—

She glanced down at her stomach, and her hand moved reflexively over the flat surface. There was a baby inside her. A baby that would need love and care and protection, despite any circumstances of its birth. A little girl, like her. Or a little boy, like Jack, who would count on Charlotte to take care of him.

She sat up straighter, knowing what she had to do.

She'd keep her pregnancy a secret—at least until the film finished shooting. The Hudsons would never have to know it had happened here. Then she could quit her job with her grandfather, and go away, somewhere private, where nobody knew her and nothing could hurt her child.

She'd have to tell Alec eventually, of course.

Alec.

Her stomach tightened with dread.

How was she going to sleep with Alec again? She couldn't do it with such a huge lie between them. And he would be back to her room, probably tonight. And she'd have to look him in the eyes and…

She groaned out loud.

"Charlotte?" It was Raine.

Charlotte grabbed at the plastic wand. "I'm…" she called out. "Just a…" She scrambled to her feet.

"Are you okay?"

"I'll be…"

But it was too late.

The en suite door was open, and Raine had crossed the bedroom.

"Cece and I were—" Raine stopped cold, with Cece nearly barreling into the back of her.

Charlotte could feel the blood drain from her face.

The cardboard package was strewn across the countertop. The wand was in her hand, with its damning positive result glaring up in living color.

Raine reached for the wand, confirming what she had already seen.

In a split second, Raine had pulled Charlotte into her arms. The dam burst loose, and Charlotte's tears flowed freely.

"It's okay," Raine crooned.

"It's a disaster," moaned Charlotte.

Raine grasped her firmly by the shoulders, pulling her slightly away, speaking firmly. "No. It's not. Babies are *never* a disaster."

"Alec doesn't want to be a father," Charlotte hiccuped. "He doesn't even want a relationship. All he wants—"

"Don't sell Alec short."

But Raine didn't understand. She had rose-colored glasses when it came to Alec. Though, who could blame her? He was a wonderful brother. He was willing to fight people for her.

The memory brought fresh tears, and the bathroom blurred around her.

She felt an arm on her shoulders, and it was Cece's voice this time. "I know how you feel," Cece stated. "I've been exactly where you are. You're scared. You feel all alone. You're desperately struggling to get your bearings."

Charlotte nodded. Cece had it exactly right.

"Now, here's what you're going to do." Cece led Charlotte to the bed, sat her down on the edge and sat next to her, taking her hand. "You are going to tell Alec immediately."

Charlotte's entire body clenched at the mere thought of that conversation.

Even Raine took a couple of reflexive steps across the bedroom. "I'm not so—"

"You have no choice," Cece continued. "You know, and he deserves to know, too."

Charlotte shook her head. It was too soon. Like Cece said, she needed to get her bearings before she did anything at all. "He doesn't need—"

"The longer you wait, the worse it gets. He'll want to know why you waited, and you will not have a good explanation."

"He doesn't need to know when I knew."

"Charlotte," said Cece with exaggerated patience, "look at me."

Charlotte did.

Raine sat down on the other side of her, rubbing one shoulder.

"I waited two years," said Cece. "First I waited a week. Then I waited two more. And then I was in Europe, and nobody had to know. And then I came back, and I had Theo to explain. I very nearly kept my son from his father."

"It won't be like that." Charlotte would tell Alec. She just needed a bit of time.

"It won't get easier," said Cece. "Every day after today, it'll get harder."

"She could be right," Raine said. "Starting the minute we walk out that door, we're all going to have to lie to him."

Cece nodded. "Can you lie to him, Charlotte?"

Charlotte shrugged, her eyes dampening again. Could she lie to Alec? She didn't want to lie to him. But she didn't want to tell him the truth, either. Because telling him the truth would mean the end. And she had so counted on things not ending just yet.

Another week. Another day. Even another night in his arms. Because once he knew, he'd never hold her tight again. He'd never whisper in her ear, nuzzle her neck, wrap his strong arms around her body. And she'd never be able to pretend, not for one more second, that they had a future together.

Not that she'd be able to pretend, anyway.

Cece was right.

She couldn't lie to Alec.

* * *

"I have to be honest," said Kiefer, as they replaced their mountain bikes in the rack in Alec's garage. "It's worse than I thought."

Alec squirted a stream of water into the back of his throat, wiping the sweat from his forehead. "You two back to fighting?" It wasn't surprising. It was damned inconvenient from a business perspective. But Alec had only himself to blame. He was the one who sent them on the trip.

Kiefer shook his head, leaning back and bracing his elbows on a workbench. "Not fighting."

"What's the problem then?" Alec didn't understand.

"All that fighting we *used* to do?"

"What?" Alec glanced at his watch. He had a conference call with Japan in an hour, and he'd hoped to see Charlotte before then.

"Turns out it was foreplay."

Alec dropped his water bottle back into the holster. "Seriously, Kiefer. Too much information. She's my sister."

Kiefer reached into his hip pocket and pulled out a small metal object, tossing it to Alec.

Alec caught it in midair. It was a scrolled silver box, hinged at the lid. He popped it open, revealing a large, diamond solitaire.

His gaze flew to Kiefer.

"It's not like I'm asking your permission or anything." Kiefer sobered. "But I wanted to give you a heads-up. I'm proposing to your sister."

"It's not about the money, is it?"

Kiefer scowled, and Alec saw a flash of genuine anger in his eyes.

"I can't believe you even asked that."

"Story of my life," said Alec.

"Not the story of mine. And you know better." Kiefer glared at him for a loaded moment.

"I know better," Alec admitted. Kiefer was a man of integrity. Alec snapped the box shut and tossed it back. His lips curved in a grin. "You think she'll say yes?"

"She damn well better," Kiefer growled. "Or else become a nun. Because that woman is never, *ever* getting near another man as long as I'm breathing."

Alec rocked forward and stuck out his hand, clasping Kiefer in a strong, thorough shake. "Then congratulations, brother. We'll talk later about reorganizing the company structure."

Kiefer held his palms up. "Hey, I'm not looking for—"

"I know you're not. But, trust me, you'll be sharing the pain the minute the honeymoon is over."

Kiefer grinned, and Alec grinned broadly in return. He couldn't imagine a better husband for Raine. He couldn't imagine a better business partner for himself.

A door opened on the far side of the garage.

Kiefer popped the ring box back in his pocket. "Better go get showered. I've got a hot date tonight."

"Good luck," said Alec. "You'll both come and see me after?"

"You bet." Kiefer gave a jaunty salute as he backed away.

"Alec?"

It was Charlotte, and Alec weaved his way through the parked cars toward her. Something deep inside him settled to contentment as he took her hands in his, drawing her into a hug.

She clung to him for a long minute, burying her head against his shoulder. But there was a tension in her body, a strain in her breathing.

He pulled back to look into her luminous, almost frightened blue eyes.

"Hey?" he asked, going on alert. "What's wrong? Your father? Jack?"

She shook her head, stepping farther away.

He reached for her, but then something held him back. He got a horrible feeling in the pit of his stomach.

"Charlotte?"

She turned her head, focusing on the small windows at the top of the bay doors where stark sunlight filtered through. "I..." She closed her eyes.

"You're scaring me," he told her honestly.

She nodded, swallowed, then looked back at him. "I'm so sorry, Alec."

"What?" He took a reflexive step forward, but she shrank back.

"Spit it out, Charlotte," he demanded. Nothing could be worse than standing here wondering what had put that look in her eyes. And nothing could be worse than getting signals that his help wasn't welcome.

"I'm—" She took a breath. "I'm pregnant."

Alec felt as though he'd been punched squarely in the gut. How could she...? When did she...?

"Who?" The question burst out of him with absolutely no eloquence whatsoever.

Her eyes squinted down. "Who what?"

"Who's the father?" He wasn't going to rail. He wasn't going to judge. She was a grown woman when she arrived on his doorstep. He hated that she had a past, but she did.

Her face contorted with anger. "How can you even *ask?*"

"You think it's none of my *business?*" Okay, now he was starting to judge. And now he was starting to get angry. He couldn't help it. The thought of another man's hands on Charlotte made him want to break something.

"You, you idiot. *You're* the father!"

Alec jerked back. "How—"

"The usual way." Her hands curled into fists by her sides.

"But it's only been—"

"Three weeks. Nearly three weeks."

"The first time?" Not bloody likely.

Her voice went hard. "I'd say so."

"We used a condom," he pointed out.

"We did."

There was a loud buzzing in his ears. She couldn't be lying. DNA tests were too easy to come by these days. She'd actually gotten herself pregnant. With his willing participation.

Here he'd thought she was different. He'd thought she was honest.

"What?" He sneered. "Did you poke holes in it?"

She blanched, but he honestly wanted to know how she'd pulled it off.

Many women had tried to trap him many different ways. He'd let his guard down with Charlotte. A mistake, obviously. But she'd seemed different, genuine, uninterested in his money. He'd been certain it was safe to enjoy a fling. But now he could almost hear his late father's admonition in his ears.

Across from him, Charlotte appeared speechless.

"What's your explanation?" he pressed.

And then they started. The big, shimmering crocodile tears he'd seen a hundred times. Next would be the protestations of innocence, the near-Oscar-quality denial that she'd been involved in any kind of plot whatsoever to get her hands on his money.

Damn.

He felt so hollow this time.

The betrayal was so much worse when he wasn't prepared.

"No explanation?" he asked.

"An accident," she managed in a halting rasp. "I didn't mean—"

"Yeah. An accidental pregnancy. Oldest trick in the book."

She shook her head.

"I guess I'll see you in court." He shook his head, turning for the door.

"Alec." His name seemed torn from her soul.

But he didn't turn back. As he made for the door, fury bubbled up inside him, both at her and at himself. He'd been a fool, and it was going to cost his family big-time.

It was all Charlotte could do to say upright. Her legs were wobbling and her broken heart was shooting pain to every corner of her being.

She'd expected to Alec to be angry.

She certainly hadn't expected him to declare his love and propose marriage. Although a small corner of her soul had hoped for that. But she hadn't expected his accusations. And she'd been completely unprepared for his cruelty.

She gripped the corner of a Mercedes. She had to walk out of here. There were a hundred people making a movie on the front lawn. Somehow, she had to hold her head up and make her way back to her room.

There, she'd pack. Hopefully, she wouldn't see anyone before she could call a taxi and make it to the airport. Home to Monte Allegro. She'd explain to her grandfather, quit her job and disappear. There was absolutely no way she'd be meeting Alec in court or anywhere else.

He could take his money and choke on it.

She heard a sound. Then Raine and Cece appeared. They rushed to her side.

"Oh, dear," said Cece.

"Bad?" asked Raine.

Charlotte nodded, valiantly fighting her tears. "I have to get back to my room. He thinks I got pregnant on purpose."

Both women gasped.

Raine growled. "I am going to—"

"No!" Charlotte grabbed Raine's arm. "Please don't say anything to him! Just let me leave. All I want to do is go home."

Raine searched Charlotte's expression for a long moment. Then she nodded. "You should go home. Take care of yourself. I'll ream my brother out later."

Alec couldn't get Charlotte's image out of his head, her tears, her confusion, her vulnerability. Obviously, she'd been certain her plan would work. Just as obviously, he couldn't let it. Even if he had been plagued with second thoughts for the past two hours.

He brought his fist down hard on the desktop.

He couldn't marry a woman who'd set him up, no matter how much he wished it could work between them. And what kind of a fool was he for even considering it?

Suddenly, his office door burst open. He spun around, ready to shout. Not even Kiefer and Raine walked in on him without knocking.

It was Jack, and before Alec could react to the shock, Jack drew back his fist.

Alec's first reaction was to duck the punch. But he forced himself to hold his ground, taking the shot straight to his jaw.

He grunted at the pain, which felt strangely good. Setup or not, he'd slept with Jack's sister and made her pregnant, and he deserved the other man's anger.

Jack stepped back, shaking out his hand, blue eyes near black with anger. "You son of a bitch," he spat.

"Yeah," Alec agreed, staring levelly into Jack's eyes.

"We'll see you in court."

Alec shook his head. "You won't have to. Your niece or nephew will have everything they could ever possibly need."

Jack snorted. "Except for a father." Then he turned for the door, and a pain worse than a cracked jaw shot through Alec.

His child would have a fractured family. Just like Charlotte. Damn.

He hated this.

He hated every single thing about it.

"Do me a favor," he called to Jack.

Jack halted. After a moment, he turned, looking ready to throw another punch.

"Tell her you decked me for it."

Jack's brow furrowed. "Why?"

Alec inhaled, taking a moment to make sure he said

it right. "Because Charlotte doesn't believe you love her. She's been waiting twenty-one years for you to start acting like a big brother."

Ten

Charlotte stared at the pile of designer clothes on the bed. Half of her wanted to forget Alec ever existed. The other half wanted to cling to every scrap of a memory.

She ran her fingertips over the gold, beaded dress she'd worn the first time they made love. Then she lifted the strap of the evening gown she'd worn to the Royal Ballet. Alec had booked the director's box, and their seats were second only to the royal family.

They'd eaten dinner overlooking the Thames, danced to an orchestra, then laughed their way through sweet treats in their bedroom at the Ritz. Alec was convinced she'd fallen in love with his lifestyle. Truth was, she'd fallen in love with Alec. She'd wear rags and live in a hut if it proved it to him.

She heard the bedroom door open, but she didn't

bother turning around. It would be Raine, back with a bigger suitcase. But it didn't matter. Charlotte had pretty much decided to leave the clothes behind.

The bed creaked, and she realized it was Jack sitting down beside her.

She hurriedly swiped her cheeks, pasting a smile on her face. "Leaving a little early," she said, gesturing to the scattered clothes. "Raine's out looking for a bigger—"

Jack's strong arm curled around her shoulders. "Oh, Charlotte."

Charlotte gasped out a sob.

Jack's other arm went around her, and he pulled her close, rocking her against his broad chest. "Cece told me. I am *so* sorry."

Charlotte shook her head, embarrassed by the fresh tears. "It's okay." She sucked a painful breath into her burning chest. "I knew… It wouldn't…" She gave up trying to talk.

Silence rose between them.

"I have loved you," Jack finally said, emotion thick in his voice, "every second of every day since they took you away from me."

Charlotte stilled.

"You were my baby sister. I thought they'd bring you back. I thought he'd—" Jack struggled with a breath. "I thought he'd come to his senses. I mean, how could anybody not love you?"

Charlotte clung to her brother, pressing her cheek against his chest while he stroked her hair. Her chest burned even more painfully. "I love you, Jack."

"I'll always love you, Charlotte. I'm here. For anything, *everything*. Whatever you need. I'm here, and Cece's here, too. And Theo. Theo will be the best cousin ever."

Charlotte nodded, a small sigh of relief coming through her wall of pain.

"I punched him out," said Jack.

Charlotte drew back.

"I punched Alec out. He doesn't mess with my baby sister and get away with it."

"Is he okay?"

Jack frowned. "Not 'thanks, big brother'?"

"Oh, yes. Thanks, big brother. But is he okay?"

Jack closed his eyes for a long second. "Uh-oh."

"What?" Not that everything wasn't colossally wrong at the moment.

"You're in love with him."

Charlotte couldn't admit it. But Jack obviously saw it in her eyes.

"Of course you're in love with him." Jack nodded. "Why else would you make love with him."

"I knew it was temporary," said Charlotte.

"But you fell for him anyway."

Charlotte closed her eyes. "Yes," she admitted quietly.

"I know how that goes," said Jack in a sympathetic tone. "When I realized I loved Cece—"

"It's not the same thing," Charlotte quickly pointed out.

"Are you sure?"

"Oh, I am sure." She nodded, voice shaking with conviction. Alec Montcalm didn't fall in love with anybody. He was honest and up-front, and he meant every syllable when he told a woman it was temporary.

"What can I do?" asked Jack.

"You can be an uncle."

He gave her another hug, and it felt good. Despite the fact that her world was falling apart, it felt so good to hug her brother again.

"I'm only a phone call away," he told her.

Charlotte glanced around. "I think I'm just going to leave. I don't need these clothes. What I need is to set up a life for a baby."

"California is nice," said Jack. "You don't have to be right in L.A. to be close by."

Charlotte managed a smile. "Thanks for that. I have to talk to the ambassador first. But I really will give it some thought." There were definitely worse places in the world than California.

Alec needed to get away, and Tokyo seemed like it might just be far enough.

He had to get Charlotte out of his head. He had to stop thinking about his baby. And he had to purge the ridiculous idea that his being in love with Charlotte, and Charlotte being in love with his money, was a recipe for happily ever after. It wasn't, and it never would be.

In the driveway, he tossed his briefcase onto the passenger seat of the Lamborghini. Then he opened the driver's door and dropped down on the seat, slamming the door and stuffing the key into the ignition.

He'd check in with Kiefer and Raine while the jet refueled in New Delhi.

"You were right," came Jack's mild voice as he appeared in Alec's rearview mirror. "She didn't know I loved her." He brought his hand down on the top of the Lamborghini's door, and rounded on Alec. "But after that, your theory fell way apart."

Alec didn't get the point. But he waited for Jack to explain.

Jack placed his other hand on the door and leaned in. "She would have given anything for it to be you who said it instead of me."

"Said what?" Alec reached for the ignition key.

"That you loved her."

Alec scoffed. That statement made absolutely no sense. "It's the money," he reminded Jack.

Jack's eyes narrowed. "Would you repeat that?"

Hell, yes. Alec would repeat it as many times as Jack liked. "Charlotte and every other woman I've ever dated are in love with my money. M-O-N-E-Y. To get it, they're willing to put up with me."

Jack suddenly looked as if he might laugh. "You actually believe that? You actually think it's the money?"

Alec didn't bother answering this time.

"Charlotte doesn't need your money," said Jack. "The family has money."

"Charlotte's not involved in Hudson Pictures." Alec knew that for a fact. Even if she hadn't told him herself, Kiefer had researched the corporation before letting them anywhere near Château Montcalm.

"I'm not talking about the Hudsons," said Jack.

What the hell else could he be talking about?

"The real money's on the Cassettes side." He shook his head as if he pitied Alec. "Charlotte is the presumptive heir to Ambassador Edmond Cassettes's fortune. And even if she wasn't, her trust fund is big enough to buy a small country."

Alec's stomach clenched around nothing.

"My God, Alec. To her, your money's probably nothing but a tax burden."

Jack might as well have slammed him in the head with a brick this time.

Charlotte had money?

Serious money?

She wasn't, *couldn't* be after Alec's.

"Then why…" He stared at Jack in confusion. What was this all about then? Why did she sleep with him? Why did she get pregnant?

Jack smacked his hands down on the car door and jerked back to standing. "Grab a clue, Alec." And he turned and walked away.

"Son of a bitch." Alec flung open the door.

None of this was making any sense. None of it. But he had to talk to Charlotte. She had to help him understand.

Charlotte came to the bottom of the main staircase with a small suitcase in her hand. Filming had finished in the foyer a few days ago, and it was back to normal again.

Raine was arranging for the limo, and Charlotte had called ahead for a plane reservation to Monte Allegro. By midnight, she'd be back in her own bed.

Then the front door burst open, and Alec strode through. Her stomach clenched, and for a second she felt a wave of dizziness.

Alec glanced from side to side. There were voices in the great room, and footsteps in the hall. On the landing above, two housekeepers chatted as they dusted the wooden railing.

Alec clenched his jaw.

He stepped determinedly forward, grasping Charlottte's hand. "Come with me."

In surprise, she dropped the suitcase, spinning around, her legs reflexively taking up a near trot as she struggled to keep up with him.

Behind the stairs, he jerked opened a thick door.

"Alec? What—" And then they were pacing down a flight of stone stairs. They rounded a corner into a cool, dimly lit wine cellar. Old racks stretched away on both sides, covered in thousands of dusty bottles of wine.

Then the aisleway widened out, revealing a hewn beam tasting table, a rack of clean glasses and several antique chairs.

Alec turned on her, letting go of her hand. "I don't understand."

Charlotte glanced around. She wasn't exactly scared, but she was more than a little confused. "I don't understand, either. What are we doing? Why did you bring me here?"

"Why did you get pregnant?"

Charlotte stood up straight, determined to maintain her composure. She had another chance to give Alec a final memory of her. And it was going to be dignified, or she would die trying.

"Did you miss eighth-grade biology?"

"That's *not* what I meant."

"Well, that's exactly how it happened. We had sex. Birth control is not foolproof, and we were in the bottom, or is it the top two percent?"

He took a few steps, in a half circle around her, eyes narrowing like a predator. "What do you want from me?"

"You're the one who dragged me down here."

"Do you want my money?"

"I never wanted your money. If you'll recall, I tried my damnedest to get you to stop spending it."

"I thought it was part of the plot." He paced back the other way.

"The *plot?*" The only plot she'd ever had was to keep away from Alec. When that became impossible, she convinced herself to have a fling. Falling for him was entirely accidental, and it would have been the stupidest plot in the world.

"To convince me you were different, so I'd let my guard down."

"Did it ever occur to you that I *was* different?"

He continued pacing. "Only every second we spent together."

"So?" What was this all about?

He came to a sudden halt. "You can't love me, Charlotte."

A chill poured over her body.

"It's not possible," he said. "It makes no sense." His expression was totally and completely sincere.

"Why not?" she dared ask.

"I'm self-centered and suspicious. I have no depth of character. And I've skated along on my family's legacy my entire life."

Charlotte couldn't believe what she was hearing.

"I accused you of sabotaging our condoms," he continued. "And, and at the time, I *meant* it." A note of desperation came into his voice. "If it's not my money— Without my money—" The question seemed torn from his soul. "What is there to love?"

Charlotte's shoulders slumped, half in astonishment and half in abject relief. "I love *you,* Alec."

He shook his head.

"I don't want your money."

"I know," he admitted.

"Then there's no other explanation, is there?"

"There could be," he argued.

She moved toward him. "Then come up with one."

He watched her in suspicious silence.

She moved in closer. "Come up with one," she dared him.

Then she stopped less than a foot away, tipping her chin to gaze at his tense expression in the dusky light. She gathered the final shreds of her courage, going for broke. "Come up with a logical explanation, or tell me that you love me back."

He stared at her, and something flickered in the depths of his dark eyes. "Are those my only choices?"

"Yeah."

"Can I propose instead?"

The burning weight lifted off Charlotte's chest, and she blinked against tears of relief. "Only if you say you love me first."

"I love you first." He reached for her. "I've loved you since I saw you on that dance floor in Rome."

"I didn't love you then," she admitted, and he laughed.

"Just so long as you caught on eventually."

"I caught on a few weeks ago." She smacked him in the shoulder. "Why weren't you paying attention?"

"Ouch." He rubbed his shoulder, pretending she'd hurt him. "You're as bad as your brother."

She peered at Alec's face. "Where'd he hit you?"

Alec pointed to his jaw.

She came up on tiptoe and kissed it better. Then she leaned forward to kiss the shoulder she'd smacked.

"I was paying attention," said Alec. "But all I could tell was that I wanted to be with you more than any other woman, other person, ever in my life. I was afraid it wasn't real." He paused. "So I guess I took steps to make sure it couldn't be real."

"It's real," she whispered, looping her arms around his neck.

His hand slipped between their bodies to rest on her stomach. "Our baby," he whispered, "is going to be loved and protected and cared for by two very happy parents."

Charlotte smiled, hope and joy flowing freely through her veins. Their baby would have loving parents, and Jack and Cece and Theo. Raine and— *Raine!*

"Raine was getting me the limo," said Charlotte. "She'll wonder—"

"Don't you worry about Raine." Alec settled his arms around Charlotte's waist. "Kiefer's taking her on a date tonight."

"That's nice." Charlotte smiled.

"He's bringing along a pretty impressive diamond solitaire."

"Really?" Charlotte was thrilled for her friend.

"He's a good man," said Alec.

She nodded in return.

"So, what about you?" he asked.

"What about me?"

He cocked his head to one side. "What are you doing tonight?"

She pretended to ponder. "Well, I do have this plane reservation."

"Canceled," he said, settling his arms more firmly at her waist.

"Then I guess I'm free."

"Care to join me for dinner?"

She smiled and pulled up for a quick kiss. "Love to."

"There's a safe in my bedroom."

"Really, Alec, condoms are no longer necess—"

He laughed. "I mean a jewelry safe."

"I thought I'd made it pretty clear that you didn't need to bribe me," she teased.

"I was thinking we could look for an engagement ring. There's no end of heirloom jewelry up there. As I recall, my grandmother— Charlotte?"

She couldn't stop her tears this time. "You were serious?"

"About marrying you? Hell, yes. Right away. Right now. As soon as we can get a license." He sobered. "You're carrying my baby, Charlotte. My heir. I'm not giving you a chance to change your mind."

"I won't change my mind," she told him sincerely. In Alec's arms for the rest of her life was exactly where she wanted to be.

In a secluded corner of the Montcalm garden, screened by cypress trees, with the scent of lavender wafting through the air, Charlotte and Alec stood next to Raine and Kiefer as the priest intoned their vows.

Charlotte wore a strapless white dress, three-quarter-length satin with flat lace over a fitted bodice, with a white satin bow tied over one hip. Raine's dress was slightly fuller, more formal, with clouds of soft tulle following to just below her knees. She had cap sleeves and a princess neckline. Both women carried bouquets of lavender and white roses.

Jack and Cece served as witnesses and, along with Theo, were the only guests. Dressed in a little gray suit, Theo played in the grass, picking wildflowers as the ceremony wore on.

Alec slipped an antique gold band onto Charlotte's

finger, snuggling it up to the two-carat, princess-cut solitaire once worn by his grandmother. As they were pronounced man and wife, he drew her to him for a long, tender kiss. When it ended, Charlotte had to force herself to let go.

Then Kiefer kissed Raine, and Jack popped the cork on the bottle of Montcalm champagne.

"Welcome to the family," Jack told Alec, pouring the pale, bubbly liquid into the waiting champagne flutes. "I trust this means we'll get a discount on renting your château?"

"Discount?" asked Alec, brows raised as Cece caught Theo's hands going for the small white and lavender wedding cake.

"Surely you won't charge your own family full price." Jack held up his glass to propose a toast.

"Surely," Kiefer echoed.

"To the brides," said Jack, his soft gaze catching Charlotte's, transporting her back to being four years old, when her big brother walked on water.

"The stunningly beautiful brides," he finished.

"The brides," the small group echoed.

"We won't charge you for the château," said Alec.

Jack nearly choked on his champagne. "I was joking," he sputtered, while Cece patted him on the back.

Charlotte gave Alec an astonished look. "But the damage."

He shrugged. "We'll—"

A loud crack rent the air, and the entire group reflexively cringed. Then something groaned, and there were far-off shouts. The wedding party rushed to the pathway in time to see Isabella, Ridley and three crew members dash out of the pool house.

A cameraman scrambled to the bottom of a stately old oak tree. The oak groaned a second time, keeling over in slow motion, falling with increasing speed until it landed on top of the pool house, squashing it flat.

David shouted something unintelligible, arms waving as he stomped toward the cameraman. But he missed a step, tripped on a cable and fell headfirst into the pool.

"Wow," said Alec, taking a sip of his champagne and resettling his arm around Charlotte's waist.

"Don't see that every day," said Kiefer.

"Yeah, that'll be coming out of David's fees," Jack put in, lifting his glass to his lips.

Charlotte anchored her arms around Alec's waist, tipping her head up. "Welcome to the family, sweetheart."

He kissed her soundly on the lips, the sweet champagne on his tongue tickling her senses and making promises for the night ahead.

He drew back, gazing into her eyes with raw longing. "And welcome to mine."

* * * * *

*Wonder what's going on
in the lives of Devlin Hudson
and his new fiancée, Valerie Shelton?
Find out in this exclusive short story by*
USA TODAY *bestselling author Maureen Child.
And be sure to look for
another story in next month's*
HUDSONS OF BEVERLY HILLS,
BARGAINED INTO HER BOSS'S BED!

Valerie Shelton walked through the production offices of Hudson Pictures and simply shook her head in amazement at the level of energy surrounding her. At every desk, someone was on the phone, gesturing wildly as if the person they were speaking to could see them. There were movie posters on the wall, the scent of stale coffee in the air and a sense of urgency that pulsed in the room like a rapid heartbeat.

She smiled to herself and realized she was excited to be a part of it all. Even just a small cog in the giant wheel that was Hudson Pictures. She was engaged to the man who made this all work. To the man who had taken her to France to see for herself the inner workings of a movie being made.

Still walking across the crowded room toward Devlin's office, Val thought back over the last week.

Their stay in Provence had been thrilling despite the fact that she and Dev hadn't gotten as close as she had hoped for.

But he was busy, she reminded herself. The man seemed to be constantly working. She admired that, even as she told herself it would change once they were married—once they were a team.

The busy room faded away as her mind took her back to the mansion in Provence where filming was taking place. The atmosphere had seemed almost magical and watching Devlin at work, seeing him handle money men and actors with the same even-handed treatment had only made her admire him more. He was a man who carried power easily. Not like her father, who ran his newspaper empire with a tight fist and a raised voice.

If there still was a small voice in the back of her mind warning her away from a man who didn't love her, she silenced it by promising herself that love would come. Eventually. She could wait. She would be the woman he wanted. The woman he needed. Until Dev finally realized that she was in his heart to stay.

After all, they'd shared at least one nearly magical moment at the château. The night before they were to fly home, they'd strolled in the darkness, their only company moonlight sliding through the thick stand of trees surrounding Alec Montcalm's estate.

"Did you have a good time?" Devlin watched her as if her answer were all too important.

"Yes," she told him, linking her arm through his. "It's exciting being behind the scenes of a movie."

He gave her a half smile and a shrug. "Exciting? Watching take after take? Hearing the actors grumble about the writing, the writers complain about rewrites and the director demanding perfection?"

"You're used to it, that's all," she said, loving the feel of his body beside hers. He was tall and strong and, in the moonlight, his blue eyes shone with wicked promise. A promise that sent her stomach in a hard spin and made heat rush through her body in response.

She hadn't thought it would be difficult to wait for sex until their wedding night, but suddenly, Val wanted Devlin to take her. To take her right there in the moonlight. She wanted them to begin their lives together in this most amazing place—to feel a connection between them that had seemed to be missing for the week they'd spent in France.

He hadn't had much time for her and though she'd expected that, she hadn't realized how hard it would be to be with him and yet apart. She'd seen how some of the film crew had watched her with sympathy in their eyes, as if they knew that she was in love—alone.

As if hearing her thoughts, Devlin stopped, turned her to face him and ran his big hands up and down her arms. He gave her a smile, and bent to press a kiss on her forehead as if she were a distant relation. "This was supposed to be a fun trip for us. I'm sorry I had to spend so much time dealing with problems."

She swallowed her disappointment. She would be the woman he needed. The woman who understood. "It's okay, really. I had a wonderful time, even though I would have liked to have more time with you."

His hands squeezed her shoulders briefly. "You're not getting much of a bargain in marrying me, Val."

Here was the man she wanted. The man who took the time to walk in the moonlight with her. The man who worried that she might regret her choice in marrying him. The annoying doubts in the back of her mind were silenced by his words and her own confidence in the decision she'd made.

"Oh, I don't know," she said, lifting one hand to lay it gently on his chest. She felt his heartbeat, slow, steady beneath her hand. "I think we'll do very well together, Dev. Here we are, in this beautiful spot, beneath the moon and right now, everything seems perfect."

He looked at her for a long thoughtful moment, and something she couldn't quite define flashed in his eyes briefly. He lifted one hand from her shoulder to cup her cheek, his thumb sliding across her skin in a caress. "You're too understanding. You know that, right?"

"Am I?"

"Yeah. Any other woman would have been complaining about being left to her own devices so often. Would have wanted to tour Provence and would have expected me to join her."

She covered his hand with hers, holding his touch to her face. "I knew this was a working trip for you, Dev…."

He studied her again, his gaze moving over her features as if committing them to memory. Then he whispered, "You really are beautiful, aren't you?"

With her hair loose around her shoulders, wearing a red, long-sleeved sweater and sleek blue jeans, she felt anything but stylish. Still, hearing him say those words fed the fires already simmering inside her.

Then he slowly lowered his head to hers. Her heartbeat kicked into a gallop, her breath stilled in her lungs and the very core of her went hot and liquid. His mouth neared hers, only a breath away now. She went up on her toes to meet him—

And his cell phone rang.

He jolted, as if lurching backward from the edge of a cliff, and mumbled, "Sorry," as he reached into his shirt pocket for the demanding phone.

Coming back to the present, Val was almost surprised to find herself standing stock-still in the middle of the production room. Her memories had been so vivid, the recollection of that near kiss in the moonlight so profound, that she'd completely lost track of where she was or what she was doing there.

Now she remembered. She'd come to surprise Devlin with a lunch date. Smiling to herself, she walked toward his office and idly noted that his assistant, a forty-something woman named Audrey, wasn't at her appointed post. Which, Val told herself, only made it easier to surprise Dev.

She strode past Audrey's desk, opened the office door and stepped inside. Devlin had his back to her, staring out the wide windows at the incredible view of Beverly Hills and the mountains beyond. Just looking at his broad back, muscles defined beneath his crisp white shirt, something inside Valerie turned over helplessly. Before she could speak, though, a disembodied voice floated out of the speakerphone on his desk.

"Looked like Val had a good time in Provence."

"Guess so," Devlin answered noncommittally.

"Well," the masculine voice countered with a half laugh, "don't get too excited."

"Let it go, Luc," Dev said and Valerie knew the man on the other end of the line was Devlin's brother Lucian. "It was what it was. A business trip. Val had a good time. I'm glad. Let it go."

"She loves you, you know."

Valerie sucked in a breath. Had she been that obvious to everyone? Was she really wearing her heart on her sleeve so openly? And was that necessarily a bad thing?

"I know," Devlin said, and turned from the window. His gaze locked with hers and a jolt of something wild and fierce and unexpected passed between them. Never taking his gaze from her, Devlin took a step toward the desk, said, "Gotta go, Luc," and clicked the disconnect button.

"Val." Devlin couldn't stop looking at her. In her trim, sleeveless green dress, she looked as cool and welcome as a cold drink at the end of a long, hot day. His body stirred and he noted his own reaction to her absently. He didn't love her, but he wanted her. That was good. Wouldn't be much of a marriage if he didn't want his wife in his bed.

The fact that she loved him worked in his favor, too, he reminded himself.

"I didn't expect to see you today."

"I thought I'd surprise you by abducting you for lunch."

He gave her a smile as he came around the edge of the desk and walked toward her. He caught her perfume in the air-conditioned office and he dragged that now-familiar scent into his lungs as he reached her. Her eyes looked huge, and he wondered if she was embarrassed to have overheard his idiot brother's comments.

"Luc didn't mean anything," he said, just in case.

"It's all right." She smiled up at him and the light in her eyes seemed to slice through him. "He wasn't wrong. I do love you, Dev. Otherwise, I wouldn't be marrying you."

Guilt tried to rear up inside him, but Devlin squashed it back down. He'd never pretended to love her, so there was no reason for guilt. With that thought firmly in mind, he mentally brushed aside the production meeting he'd scheduled for lunch.

He didn't love the woman he was about to marry, but that didn't mean he couldn't give her what she needed once in a while.

"Lunch is a great idea," he said, turning from her to go snag his suit jacket off the hanger in his closet. Slipping it on, he walked back to her, took her hand and threaded her arm through his. The touch of her skin sent a scorching need of lust staggering through him and Devlin welcomed it. Need he could deal with. Lust was welcome. Love wasn't on the table. "What do you think? The Ivy?"

"Really?" Her pleased smile lit up her face and, just for a second, Devlin thought about letting her go for her own sake. Letting her find someone who would be able to love her back. But then he remembered why he was marrying her. The Shelton newspaper dynasty and Hudson Pictures were going to be a great team. Best to keep that in mind.

"You're not too busy?"

Shaking his head to clear his wandering thoughts, he gave her a smile. "I think Hollywood can get along without me for an hour or so."

* * * * *

*Celebrate 60 years of pure
reading pleasure with Harlequin®!*
*Silhouette® Romantic Suspense is celebrating
with the glamour-filled, adrenaline-charged series*
LOVE IN 60 SECONDS
starting in April 2009.
*Six stories that promise to bring
the glitz of Las Vegas, the danger of revenge,
the mystery of a missing diamond, family scandals
and ripped-from-the-headlines intrigue.
Get your heart racing
as love happens in sixty seconds!*

Enjoy a sneak peek of
USA TODAY *bestselling author*
Marie Ferrarella's
THE HEIRESS'S 2-WEEK AFFAIR
*Available April 2009
from Silhouette® Romantic Suspense.*

Eight years ago Matt Shaffer had vanished out of Natalie Rothchild's life, leaving behind a one-line note tucked under a pillow that had grown cold: *I'm sorry, but this just isn't going to work.*

That was it. No explanation, no real indication of remorse. The note had been as clinical and compassionless as an eviction notice, which, in effect, it had been, Natalie thought as she navigated through the morning traffic. Matt had written the note to evict her from his life.

She'd spent the next two weeks crying, breaking down without warning as she walked down the street, or as she sat staring at a meal she couldn't bring herself to eat.

Candace, she remembered with a bittersweet pang, had tried to get her to go clubbing in order to get her to forget about Matt.

She'd turned her twin down, but she did get her act

together. If Matt didn't think enough of their relationship to try to contact her, to try to make her understand
why he'd changed so radically from lover to stranger,
then to hell with him. He was dead to her, she resolved.
And he'd remained that way.

Until twenty minutes ago.

The adrenaline in her veins kept mounting.

Natalie focused on her driving. Vegas in the daylight wasn't nearly as alluring, as magical and glitzy
as it was after dark. Like an aging woman best seen in
soft lighting, Vegas's imperfections were all visible in
the daylight. Natalie supposed that was why people
like her sister didn't like to get up until noon. They
lived for the night.

Except that Candace could no longer do that.

The thought brought a fresh, sharp ache with it.

"Damn it, Candy, what a waste," Natalie murmured
under her breath.

She pulled up before the Janus casino. One of the
three valets currently on duty came to life and made a
beeline for her vehicle.

"Welcome to the Janus," the young attendant said
cheerfully as he opened her door with a flourish.

"We'll see," she replied solemnly.

As he pulled away with her car, Natalie looked up
at the casino's logo. Janus was the Roman god with
two faces, one pointed toward the past, the other
facing the future. It struck her as rather ironic, given
what she was doing here, seeking out someone from
her past in order to get answers so that the future could
be settled.

The moment she entered the casino, the Vegas phe-
nomena took hold. It was like stepping into a world

where time did not matter or even make an appearance. There was only a sense of "now."

Because in Natalie's experience she'd discovered that bartenders knew the inner workings of any establishment they worked for better than anyone else, she made her way to the first bar she saw within the casino.

The bartender in attendance was a gregarious man in his early forties. He had a quick, sexy smile, which was probably one of the main reasons he'd been hired. His name tag identified him as Kevin.

Moving to her end of the bar, Kevin asked, "What'll it be, pretty lady?"

"Information." She saw a dubious look cross his brow. To counter that, she took out her badge. Granted she wasn't here in an official capacity, but Kevin didn't need to know that. "Were you on duty last night?"

Kevin began to wipe the gleaming black surface of the bar. "You mean during the gala?"

"Yes."

The smile gracing his lips was a satisfied one. Last night had obviously been profitable for him, she judged. "I caught an extra shift."

She took out Candace's photograph and carefully placed it on the bar. "Did you happen to see this woman there?"

The bartender glanced at the picture. Mild interest turned to recognition. "You mean Candace Rothchild? Yeah, she was here, loud and brassy as always. But not for long," he added, looking rather disappointed. There was always a circus when Candace was around, Natalie thought. "She and the boss had at it and then he had our head of security escort her out."

She latched on to the first part of his statement. "They argued? About what?"

He shook his head. "Couldn't tell you. Too far away for anything but body language," he confessed.

"And the head of security?" she asked.

"He got her to leave."

She leaned in over the bar. "Tell me about him."

"Don't know much," the bartender admitted. "Just that his name's Matt Shaffer. Boss flew him in from L.A. where he was head of security for Montgomery Enterprises."

There was no avoiding it, she thought darkly. She was going to have to talk to Matt. The thought left her cold. "Do you know where I can find him right now?"

Kevin glanced at his watch. "He should be in his office. On the second floor, toward the rear." He gave her the numbers of the rooms where the monitors that kept watch over the casino guests as they tried their luck against the house were located.

Taking out a twenty, she placed it on the bar. "Thanks for your help."

Kevin slipped the bill into his vest pocket. "Anytime, lovely lady," he called after her. "Anytime."

She debated going up the stairs, then decided on the elevator. The car that took her up to the second floor was empty. Natalie stepped out of the elevator, looked around to get her bearings and then walked toward the rear of the floor.

"Into the Valley of Death rode the six hundred," she silently recited, digging deep for a line from a poem by Tennyson. Wrapping her hand around a brass handle, she opened one of the glass doors and walked in.

The woman whose desk was closest to the door

looked up. "You can't come in here. This is a restricted area."

Natalie already had her ID in her hand and held it up. "I'm looking for Matt Shaffer," she told the woman.

God, even saying his name made her mouth go dry. She was supposed to be over him, to have moved on with her life. What happened?

The woman began to answer her. "He's—"

"Right here."

The deep voice came from behind her. Natalie felt every single nerve ending go on tactical alert at the same moment that all the hairs at the back of her neck stood up. Eight years had passed, but she would have recognized his voice anywhere.

* * * * *

Why did Matt Shaffer leave
heiress-turned-cop Natalie Rothchild?
What does he know about
the death of Natalie's twin sister?
Come and meet these two reunited lovers
and learn the secrets of the Rothchild family in
THE HEIRESS'S 2-WEEK AFFAIR
by USA TODAY bestselling author
Marie Ferrarella.
The first book in Silhouette® Romantic Suspense's
wildly romantic new continuity,
LOVE IN 60 SECONDS!
Available April 2009.

CELEBRATE
60 YEARS
OF PURE READING PLEASURE
WITH **HARLEQUIN**®!

Look for Silhouette®
Romantic Suspense in April!

Love In 60 Seconds

Bright lights. Big city. Hearts in overdrive.

Silhouette® Romantic Suspense is celebrating
Harlequin's 60th Anniversary with six stories that
promise to bring readers the glitz of Las Vegas,
the danger of revenge, the mystery of a missing
diamond, and family scandals.

**Look for the first title, *The Heiress's 2-Week Affair*
by *USA TODAY* bestselling author
Marie Ferrarella, on sale in April!**

His 7-Day Fiancée by **Gail Barrett**	May
The 9-Month Bodyguard by **Cindy Dees**	June
Prince Charming for 1 Night by **Nina Bruhns**	July
Her 24-Hour Protector by **Loreth Anne White**	August
5 minutes to Marriage by **Carla Cassidy**	September

---

www.eHarlequin.com   SRS60BPA

You're invited to join our Tell Harlequin Reader Panel!

By joining our new reader panel you will:

- Receive Harlequin® books—they are FREE and yours to keep with no obligation to purchase anything!
- Participate in fun online surveys
- Exchange opinions and ideas with women just like you
- Have a say in our new book ideas and help us publish the best in women's fiction

In addition, you will have a chance to win great prizes and receive special gifts!
See Web site for details. Some conditions apply.
Space is limited.

To join, visit us at
www.TellHarlequin.com.

THBPA0108

Silhouette

nocturne BITES

**Dark, sexy and not quite human.
Introducing a collection of
new paranormal short stories
by top Nocturne authors.**

Look for the first collection—

MIDNIGHT CRAVINGS

**Featuring Werewolf and Hellhound stories
from
MICHELE HAUF, KAREN WHIDDON,
LORI DEVOTI, ANNA LEONARD,
VIVI ANNA and BONNIE VANAK.**

**Indulge in Nocturne Bites
beginning in April 2009.**

Available wherever books are sold.

www.silhouettenocturne.com
www.paranormalromanceblog.wordpress.com

SNBITES09R

REQUEST YOUR FREE BOOKS!

2 FREE NOVELS PLUS 2 FREE GIFTS!

Silhouette® Desire®

Passionate, Powerful, Provocative!

YES! Please send me 2 FREE Silhouette Desire® novels and my 2 FREE gifts (gifts are worth about $10). After receiving them, if I don't wish to receive any more books, I can return the shipping statement marked "cancel". If I don't cancel, I will receive 6 brand-new novels every month and be billed just $4.05 per book in the U.S. or $4.74 per book in Canada, plus 25¢ shipping and handling per book and applicable taxes, if any*. That's a savings of almost 15% off the cover price! I understand that accepting the 2 free books and gifts places me under no obligation to buy anything. I can always return a shipment and cancel at any time. Even if I never buy another book, the two free books and gifts are mine to keep forever.

225 SDN ERVX 326 SDN ERVM

Name	(PLEASE PRINT)	
Address		Apt. #
City	State/Prov.	Zip/Postal Code

Signature (if under 18, a parent or guardian must sign)

Mail to the **Silhouette Reader Service:**
IN U.S.A.: P.O. Box 1867, Buffalo, NY 14240-1867
IN CANADA: P.O. Box 609, Fort Erie, Ontario L2A 5X3

Not valid to current subscribers of Silhouette Desire books.

Want to try two free books from another line?
Call 1-800-873-8635 or visit www.morefreebooks.com.

* Terms and prices subject to change without notice. N.Y. residents add applicable sales tax. Canadian residents will be charged applicable provincial taxes and GST. Offer not valid in Quebec. This offer is limited to one order per household. All orders subject to approval. Credit or debit balances in a customer's account(s) may be offset by any other outstanding balance owed by or to the customer. Please allow 4 to 6 weeks for delivery. Offer available while quantities last.

Your Privacy: Silhouette Books is committed to protecting your privacy. Our Privacy Policy is available online at www.eHarlequin.com or upon request from the Reader Service. From time to time we make our lists of customers available to reputable third parties who may have a product or service of interest to you. If you would prefer we not share your name and address, please check here. ☐

SDES08R

Did you enjoy meeting Terrence Jeffries?
Don't miss his steamy story…

Temperatures Rising

**NEW YORK TIMES
BESTSELLING AUTHOR**

BRENDA JACKSON

Radio producer Sherrie Griffin
is used to hot, stormy weather.
But the chemistry between her
and sports DJ Terrence Jeffries
is a new kind of tempest.
Stranded together during a
Florida hurricane, they take
shelter…in each other's arms.

Book 1 of the
Mother Nature Matchmaker
series

Available May 2009 wherever books are sold.

**www.kimanipress.com
www.myspace.com/kimanipress**

KPDBJMAR09

HARLEQUIN®

INTRIGUE®

B.J. DANIELS

FIVE BROTHERS

ONE MARRIAGE-PACT
RACE TO THE HITCHING POST

MONTANA

The Corbetts

SHOTGUN BRIDE

Available April 2009

Catch all five adventures in
this new exciting miniseries
from B.J. Daniels!

www.eHarlequin.com   HI69392

COMING NEXT MONTH
Available April 14, 2009

#1933 THE UNTAMED SHEIK—Tessa Radley
Man of the Month
Whisking a suspected temptress to his desert palace seems the only way to stop her…until unexpected attraction flares and he discovers she may not be what he thought after all.

#1934 BARGAINED INTO HER BOSS'S BED—Emilie Rose
The Hudsons of Beverly Hills
He'll do anything to get what he wants—including seduce his assistant to keep her from quitting!

#1935 THE MORETTI SEDUCTION—Katherine Garbera
Moretti's Legacy
This charming tycoon has never heard the word *no*—until now. Attracted to his business rival, he finds himself in a fierce battle both in the boardroom…and the bedroom.

#1936 DAKOTA DADDY—Sara Orwig
Stetsons & CEOs
Determined to buy a ranch from his former lover and family rival, he's shocked to discover he's a father! Now he'll stop at nothing short of seduction to get his son.

#1937 PRETEND MISTRESS, BONA FIDE BOSS—
Yvonne Lindsay
Rogue Diamonds
His plan had been to proposition his secretary into being his companion for the weekend. But he *didn't* plan on wanting more than just a business relationship….

#1938 THE HEIR'S SCANDALOUS AFFAIR—
Jennifer Lewis
The Hardcastle Progeny
When the mysterious woman he spent a passionate night with returns to tell him he may be a Hardcastle, he wonders what a Hardcastle man should do to get her back in his bed.

SDCNMBPA0309